TRICK ME

IMMORTAL VICES AND VIRTUES: SHADOW SHIFTER BONDS

A STANDALONE NOVELLA

MILA YOUNG

CONTENTS

Wicked Game

Talia Lahoud

Fireline Heart

Asiq

Forgive Me Father

Drayce Music

Does He?

Ruby Darkrose

Bad Dreams

Teddy Swims

Golden

KPop Demon Hunters Cast

Ordinary

Alex Warren

Lose Control

Teddy Swims

Click Here To Listen To The Soundtrack

PROLOGUE

Death smells like peppermint and regret, at least when it's wearing an expensive suit and trying to buy forgiveness for cheating on his wife before he died.

"She needs to know about the Cyprus account," the ghost insists, his translucent form flickering like bad reception on an old television. He's still wearing the same charcoal suit he died in, though the three bullet holes add a certain *je ne sais quoi* to the ensemble. The bloodstains have gone rusty brown in death. Funny how ghosts keep the worst parts of how they died but lose all the good stuff, like being able to actually touch the people they're haunting.

I'm wrapped in three sweaters despite it being August in Helsinki, my breath misting in the consultation room's suddenly arctic air. The cold is always the first price I pay for my ability to speak to the dead, and my body temperature drops with every second I hold the connection open. By the end of an hour session, I'll be shaking like a chihuahua in a freezer.

"Your husband wants you to know about Cyprus," I tell Mrs. Lindqvist, trying to keep my teeth from chattering. The consultation room is painted in what our decorator called Soothing Sage, but right now it looks more like Institutional Prison Green. The mahogany table and the chairs are some ergonomic nightmare that's supposed to promote spiritual open-ness. Mostly they promote back pain.

Mrs. Lindqvist sits ramrod straight, her face pulled so tight from surgical enhancements that I'm genuinely concerned she might crack if she tries to frown. She's dripping in diamonds that could fund a small country's revolution, from earrings to a necklace to rings on seven of her ten fingers. Her platinum blonde hair is shellacked into a helmet that could probably stop bullets, which is ironic considering her husband didn't have the same protection.

"Cyprus?" She leans forward, the bridge of her nose scrunching up. "We never went to Cyprus."

The ghost, Mr. Erik Lindqvist, former black-market artifact dealer, current pain in my frozen ass, waves his arms frantically. His edges blur when he gets emotional, like someone is smudging him with an eraser. "The account! Tell her about the account! Three million euros! The password is her mother's maiden name!"

"He says there's an account there. Three million. Password is your mother's maiden name."

Her eyes narrow to slits. "My mother's maiden name or that whore's mother's maiden name?"

Erik flinches. Even dead, he knows he's in trouble. "Tell her it wasn't like that—"

"He says it's not—" I dutifully relay but am interrupted.

"Then what was it like?" Her voice is venom, staring at me and then at the room around her, never quite in his direction. "When he was meeting with that artifact broker? When she was evaluating his collection? When her boyfriend put three bullets in his chest?"

Erik's form solidifies, and suddenly he's easier to see—the web of broken capillaries across his nose from too much expensive whiskey, the soft jaw of a man who hired others to do his dangerous work, the manicured hands that most likely never did the hard tasks. In death, all our pretty lies become transparent.

"She seduced me!" he wails. "It was a trap from the beginning! Tell her—"

The cold suddenly spikes, frost spreading across the table's polished surface. My nose starts bleeding, another fun side effect of channeling the dead for too long. The crimson drops freeze before they hit my lap. I quickly grab a tissue from the box on the table.

"Mr. Lindqvist says..." I pause, dabbing at my nose. "He insists it was a trap."

"Yeah, right!" Mrs. Lindqvist's laugh is ear-piercing. "Is that what he's calling it when he thinks with his—"

Erik's ghost suddenly rushes forward, and his form shifts into something altogether less human. His face elongates, jaw unhinging like a snake's, empty eye sockets weeping black mist. This is what happens when spirits get too emotional—they stop pretending to be human and show what death really looks like underneath.

"TELL HER I'M SORRY!" His voice layers, becoming a harmony of screams. "TELL HER ABOUT THE MONEY SHE CAN HAVE! TELL HER—"

I slam my hand on the table. "Silence. Please."

The room goes quiet except for my ragged breathing. Erik shrinks back to his human shape, looking petulant. Mrs. Lindqvist can't see any of this, of course. She just sees me, pale and bleeding and probably looking like I'm having a stroke.

"Perhaps," I manage through chattering teeth. "We should continue this next week. The connection is... unstable today."

"What does that mean?" Mrs. Lindqvist clutches her bag like she wants to beat someone with it. Probably me. "I'm paying two thousand gold coins and blood for this."

And I'm literally freezing my soul off for your marital drama, I think but don't say. Customer service, even for the dead and their insufferable widows.

"Spirits don't... process emotions the same way after crossing over," I explain, the lie rolling smooth as silk off my tongue. Truth is, some spirits are just assholes; death didn't improve them any. "Your husband seems quite agitated. It might be better to let him settle."

She stands abruptly, the chair scraping against the imported marble floor. "Next week, I want real answers. About the rest of the money. About her. About everything."

"Of course," I say, though what I'm thinking is *Maybe try a therapist instead of a medium, lady.*

She storms out, her heels clicking on the marble. The door, heavy oak with sound-dampening spells woven into the grain, closes with a whisper instead of a slam. We paid extra for that feature after too many clients tried to dramatically exit.

Erik's ghost hovers there, looking like a kicked puppy. If puppies were transparent and had bullet holes.

"She never appreciated what I did for her," he moans.

"You mean like dying on the day you were

renewing your vows with her?" I ask, finally free to speak my mind.

"I was murdered! Otherwise, I was careful."

"You were a sixty-year-old man having an affair with a woman younger than your daughter. That's not careful. That's a midlife crisis with a death wish." I stand, my legs shaking from the cold. "Now get out. I have other dead people to deal with, and at least some of them have the decency to be interesting."

Erik's ghost vanishes with a pop of displaced air. The temperature in the room immediately rises ten degrees, though I'm still shivering. I breathe easier.

I make my way out of the consultation room and into the main floor of what we call the Nordic Institute of Posthumous Communications. We mostly just call it the Institute, or as I prefer, the Office Where Dreams Go to Die and Then Complain About It.

Some of the interns started calling it NIPS, which, unfortunately, stuck, much like the ghosts in the elevator shaft.

The building didn't exist before the portals opened, and society restructured itself around magic instead of money a long time ago. Well, magic *and* gold. Some things never change. The main floor soars three stories high, with art deco fixtures that someone decided to *improve* with floating light orbs that shift color based on the spiritual energy in the room. Right now they're a sickly yellow, which means someone is having a bad day with their particular brand of death magic.

There are lines of meeting pods for our less dramatic consultations. We have a vault, reinforced with enough protective spells to stop a magical attack, that holds cursed objects we're either studying or waiting to destroy. And my desk, along with thirty others, sits in an open office.

Most things in the office run on magic, giving us the use of some technologies many around the world don't have.

My desk is a standing model that adjusts to height. We have a varied staff, from a pixie in Accounting who tops out at three feet to a half giant in Security who has to duck through doorways. The surface is black glass that displays my calendar, active cases, and approximately seventeen different warning systems for spiritual intrusions.

I collapse into my chair, pulling my sweaters tighter. August in Helsinki is usually warm enough that normal people are in sundresses and shorts. I'm dressed like I'm about to climb Everest, and I'm still cold. The Institute keeps my area at a balmy twenty-eight degrees Celsius, but when you're channeling the dead, your body temperature drops to match theirs.

"Rough session?"

Dmitri looks up from his desk, where he's examining what appears to be a jewelry box wrapped in chains. As a curse breaker, he deals with objects that want to kill, maim, or occasionally turn people inside out. The hazard pay is excellent. The mortality rate is... not.

He's unfairly attractive in that carved-from-marble way that has you wanting to either paint him or lick him. Sharp cheekbones, white-blond hair that he keeps tied back while working, and eyes like winter ice. He's also wearing thick leather gloves that go up to his elbows and a protective apron covered in runes, which somewhat ruins the aesthetic. On the table in front of him sits a transparent half orb of magic, barely visible except for the occasional glint of light. His hands are buried inside it, working around the sealed box like it might bite.

"Lindqvist case again," I say, not bothering to elaborate. Everyone knows about them. The Institute loves these high-profile cases because they pay well. I hate them because the dead are usually assholes, and the living are worse.

Next appointment in twenty minutes. "And before you ask, no, it's still not resolved, and she's returning next week."

"The dead don't exactly feel compelled to kiss and tell." That's not entirely true. Sometimes they won't shut up about their conquests. But Erik seems more concerned with making it up to his wife.

Dmitri goes back to his work, and across from me,

Marcus is chatting with a manager about what sounds like a haunted house situation, before the boss man leaves. The other desks are empty right now.

We all live in the House of Gold and Garnet, which rules our corner of the world, demanding excellence in all things. We're the cleanup crew for the aftermath of magic, the ones who deal with what happens when spells go wrong, when the dead won't stay dead, when curses take root and spread.

When the portals in our world first opened to a world ruled by humans and magic flooded in like a tsunami, the majority of humanity died in the first wave. The survivors either adapted, evolved, or got very good at hiding. Then the world slowly divided into Houses, taking control over various countries and seas.

These Houses now rule what's left of the world, each seeming to attract a certain type of magic and supernaturals. And in the House of Gold and Garnet, we got death, wealth, and violence. We're the dangerous side of the world, the flashy, profitable, and hiding-bodies-in-the-basement kind. Our territory stretches across several countries, all under the rule of King Kaspian, who governs from his modern palace in Reykjavík. They say he bathes in blood and eats diamonds for breakfast. They say a lot of things. All I know is our pay each month clears.

The Institute is one of the crown jewels of our

House's death services. We handle everything from simple hauntings to mass possessions, from curse breaking to spiritual negotiations. And then there's me, the only natural medium in the Institute who doesn't need rituals, blood sacrifice, or machinery to talk to the dead.

Lucky me.

The Institute found me three years ago during what the newspapers called "The Helsinki Library Disaster." I was studying, minding my own business in the library, when the construction crew breaking ground on the new wing hit something they shouldn't have.

Turns out there was a mass grave under the library. Viking raiders from a long time ago, buried without proper rites, their spirits bound to the earth by violence and rage. When the construction crew's drill hit the first skull, all forty-three Vikings woke up at once.

And they were pissed.

Twenty-three students started speaking in Old Norse, warning about blood and vengeance. The temperature dropped so fast that the windows shattered. Books flew off shelves, forming words in languages that had been dead for centuries. And me? I was the only one who could see them, all forty-three Viking warriors in full battle gear, axes raised, ready to possess every living soul in a three-block radius.

I don't remember much of what happened next. The security footage showed me rising four feet off the ground, my eyes going solid white, speaking fluent Old Norse despite never studying it. I bound all forty-three spirits and sent them to their rest, but not before every camera in the area caught me looking like something out of a horror movie.

The Institute's recruiters got to me fast. Offered me a salary I couldn't refuse.

My calendar pings. Next appointment in fifteen minutes with a CEO who wants to know if his business partner is really dead or just faking it for the insurance money. These are my favorite cases. Half the time, the ghost is actually just a very much alive person hiding.

The pneumatic tube beside my desk makes its distinctive whoosh. The Institute loves them, and they're powered by compressed air spirits (don't ask) and can deliver anything from case files to coffee orders anywhere in the building. They painted them brass and added unnecessary gears because someone in Facilities Management has read too many adventure novels about old airships and clockwork.

I'm expecting case files.

Instead, a black envelope with a gold seal lands on my desk. It's a serpent eating its own tail, picked out in gold wax. I break the seal.

The whisper starts immediately, not in my ears but

in my bones: *The frozen heart seeks flame. The burning soul seeks ice.*

Strange, but I often hear voices and have become accustomed to ignoring them.

Inside, the invitation is written on translucent parchment with glittering black text. It features the serpent logo at the top and reads...

A night of mischief, magic, and mayhem awaits you. You are cordially invited to the first All Hallows' Eve Ball at Crossroads. Arrive by the stroke of ten, dressed in your finest enchantments, or forfeit your place. Masks are optional. Secrets are not.

See you soon, Erynn Mäkinen.

Coordinates are included on the back of the invitation.

I stare at the invitation, at the serpent insignia, my mind racing. The logo belongs to Vaelora. Everyone knows about her, even if no one I know has actually met her. She's a mysterious fae who recently arrived at Cross-roads, a few months after the portal opened. She's known for being extremely powerful and throwing grand, seductive events that are full of magic, inviting a variety of random people. Rumors say that no one declines her invitations... These are parties you will never forget.

"Fuck me sideways, you got one too?"

I nearly jump out of my skin. Sera perches on my desk like she owns it, which, knowing Sera, she probably thinks she does. She's the Institute's emergency response specialist, a blood witch who can stop a rampaging revenant with three drops of virgin blood and a dirty limerick.

Today she's wearing a leather pencil skirt and a silk blouse the color of fresh blood that brings out the burgundy in her hair. Her lips are painted the exact shade, and her nails are sharp.

She's also my best friend, and I absolutely adore her.

"Tell me that's not what I think it is," I say, nodding at the matching black envelope in her hand.

"Invitation to Vaelora's ball? The party everyone whispers about but no one admits attending? The event that supposedly changes your life forever?" Sera grins, and her canines are just a little too sharp to be human. "Oh, yeah, baby. We're going to party with the fae."

"No." I shake my head. "I haven't decided if I'm going yet."

"When was the last time you went out?" Sera asks, examining her nails like she's not about to emotionally manipulate me.

"I went to the store last week."

"Doesn't count."

"There were people there."

"Living people?"

I pause. "The security guard. Probably. He was very solid-looking."

Sera hops off my desk and leans over, dropping her head to the top of it dramatically. "You're going to die alone, surrounded by ghosts who are probably terrible conversationalists."

I notice that Dmitri is getting up and leaving his desk, and I feel it has everything to do with our loud conversation.

"They're not so bad," I answer Sera. "They have literally nothing but time."

"Erynn." She looks up, and there's something serious in her expression. "Rich might be there."

Ah. Richard. Sera's on-again, off-again whatever-he-is. Tall, dark, and handsome in that I-definitely-kill-people-for-money way. He disappears for months at a time, comes back with expensive gifts, and rocks Sera's world just long enough to make her stupid before vanishing again.

"He's been gone for two months," she continues. "This is exactly the kind of place he'd resurface. All mysterious and dangerous and—"

"And toxic," I interrupt. "Sera, he treats you like a pit stop between murder tours."

"I know." She sighs. "But gods, Erynn, you should see what that man can do with his tongue. I swear he's part demon. The things he does to my—"

"And we're done with that conversation," Marcus

calls from his desk, not looking up from his computer. "Some of us are trying to eat lunch."

"It's ten in the morning," Sera points out.

"I had an early start."

"Anyway, Rich isn't my actual boyfriend," Sera explains automatically. "He's my... complicated sexual arrangement and rare emotional vulnerability."

"That's actually worse," I tell her.

She sighs. "I know." She turns back to me, and now she's in full pleading mode. "Please come with me? Please? I need moral support. And someone to keep me from doing something stupid when Rich shows up looking all brooding and dangerous."

"You're going to do something stupid regardless."

"Yes, but with you there, I'll at least feel guilty about it."

I look down at the invitation. The serpent seal seems to wink at me, which is disturbing on multiple levels. The whisper echoes in my mind: *Stay away*.

I try one last time. "I have four clients booked on Halloween, so I can't really go."

"Cancel them. Tell them the dead will still be dead next week."

"That's terrible customer service."

"You know what's horrible? Your social life. When was the last time you got laid?"

Marcus makes a choking sound. "And that's my

cue to take an early break." He practically runs for the elevator.

"Sera—"

"Six months? A year?"

"I don't—"

"Two years?" Her eyes widen. "Oh my, it's been more than two years, hasn't it?"

"Can we not—"

She leans in. "Your vagina is going to seal shut. Like, literally close for business. Put up a little Closed Indefinitely sign."

"That's not how anatomy works."

"It is when you ignore it for that long. Trust me, I'm a blood witch. I know things about bodies."

"You know how to explode them, not maintain them."

"Same principle." She leans even closer, grabbing my hands. Her skin is always fever-warm, a side effect of all the blood magic. "Please. One night. Wear something pretty, drink something irresponsible, maybe talk to someone who has a pulse. What's the worst that could happen?"

At a fae party at Crossroads on Halloween?

My imagination immediately supplies about seventeen different scenarios, each worse than the last. Everything from being turned into a toad to having my soul stolen to ending up in a different dimension where everything is made of teeth.

But Sera is staring at me with those big emerald eyes, and I can feel the invitation pulse in my hand like a heartbeat.

"Fine," I say, already regretting it. "But I'm not wearing anything ridiculous."

"Yes!" Sera literally bounces. "This is going to be amazing! I have the perfect dress for you. It's a shimmery blue, and it's going to look like you have nothing to do with death."

I arch a brow, but she's already too deep in the fantasy to notice. Her excitement is practically vibrating off her, and damn it, I've never been good at resisting her when she gets like this, sparkling eyes, wild gestures, the whole manic friend thing in full force. My resolve wavers.

"The point is, you're going to look hot, and we're going to find someone to break your dry spell."

I snort. "I don't have a—"

"Two years, Erynn. Two. Years. You admitted it."

I hold up my hands in protest but decide it's easier to surrender, as she isn't going to let this go. "Okay. But if something goes horribly wrong, I'm blaming you."

"It's just a party."

I think about Mrs. Lindqvist and her dead husband, about the ghosts that sometimes crowd around me when I'm in old places. About two years of nothing but work and sleep and the occasional conversation with someone who doesn't have a pulse.

Maybe change isn't the worst thing that could happen.

Maybe it's exactly what I need.

I tuck the invitation into my desk drawer. "We're going to a party."

Sera squeals and hugs me, and I pretend not to notice that the temperature in the room drops five degrees.

After all, what's the worst that could happen at a Halloween party thrown by a fae?

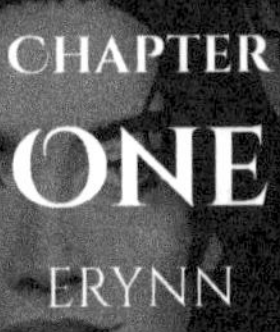

The portal spits us out like we're last week's leftovers, and I immediately regret wearing heels.

"Hell," Sera gasps, catching herself on a tree that definitely wasn't there five seconds ago. "Every single time. You'd think after three years of portal travel, I'd remember to brace for the landing."

"You literally arranged this," I remind her, trying to find my balance on moss that glows a concerning shade of blue where my stilettos sink in. "You said, and I quote, 'I've got the perfect portal spell, much smoother than the commercial ones.'"

"I may have oversold my abilities." She straightens, brushing imaginary dirt off her dress. "But look at us. We're here, we're gorgeous, and we're only mildly traumatized from interdimensional travel."

She's not wrong about the gorgeous part. Sera's outfit is pure sin meets dark fairy tale. A corseted top in black leather that looks like it was poured onto her, intricate lacing up the back that probably took her an hour to get into. The skirt is layers of burgundy tulle and black lace that move like smoke when she walks, short in the front, longer in the back, revealing thigh-high boots with lots of buckles. Her hair is piled high, and her lips are painted such a dark red that they're almost black.

"You look like you eat men's souls for breakfast," I tell her. "You're absolutely stunning, babe."

She giggles. "Only on special days. Weekends, I'm a vegetarian." She gives me a once-over and whistles low. "Speaking of souls, you're going to steal a few tonight yourself."

The dress she forced me into is nothing I would have chosen for myself. Ice-blue silk that feels like wearing water, with a single strap over my left shoulder, while the right side is completely bare. The fabric clings to me, and the slit on the left goes high. My hair is down in soft waves she created with heated stones and potions that smelled like winter roses and something burnt, falling past my shoulders. I adjust my gold thin necklace with a crescent moon. We both wear lacy black eye masks for the Halloween vibe.

"You did amazing with picking this dress for me," I

admit, grinning. It's not often I get the chance to dress up.

"Very 'touch me and die, but maybe the death would be worth it' look."

"That's not a thing."

"It is now."

Around us, the forest is something out of a dark fairy tale. Trees with silver bark that seems to pulse with its own light, shadows that move independently of their sources, and that blue-glowing moss that's either magical or radioactive. Other guests are materializing from their own portals. A couple appears in a shower of golden sparks, and a group of three stumbles out of what looks like a tear in reality itself.

"Look." Sera points ahead to where flowers are beginning to glow along a previously invisible path.

We begin our walk forward. "Can you hear that?" I ask.

Music drifts through the trees—string instruments, drums, and something that might be singing, but in no language I recognize.

"I feel it," Sera adds, and she's right. The music isn't just auditory; it's tugging at something behind my ribs.

More people pass us on the path—a woman whose dress appears to be made of actual shadows that trail behind her like smoke, a man in a mask shaped like a wolf skull that covers his entire head, twins in matching silver who move in perfect synchronization like they're sharing one mind.

"We're underdressed," I whisper.

"No, we fit in perfectly," Sera corrects. "We just haven't had three centuries to perfect our aesthetic like some of these people."

We emerge from the tree line, and my brain short-circuits trying to process what I'm seeing.

The mansion doesn't just sprawl; it conquers. It rises from the ground like it was grown rather than built, all towers and turrets and walls that shift between stone and starlight, maybe, or crystallized moonlight. The full moon overhead is wrong, too large and too bright, casting shadows that fall in directions that shouldn't be possible.

"That's... that's not architecturally possible," I manage.

"Nothing about this place is possible. That's the point." Sera grabs my arm. "Come on, I need to see this place."

Enormous iron gates stand open, and the moment we pass through them, the temperature changes so dramatically that I gasp. From forest cold to perfect warmth in a single step.

"Magic climate control," Sera says appreciatively. "Do you have any idea how much power that takes?"

"Enough to make our host someone we definitely don't want to piss off?"

"Exactly."

The driveway curves toward the mansion, and I stop again at the sight of the fountain. Three tiers of what looks like black glass but moves like liquid. Lights dance beneath the surface.

A group ahead of us has stopped to take in the fountain as well, all wearing elaborate masks. A woman in a peacock mask turns to look at us, and I realize her eyes behind the mask are completely gold, no whites, no pupils. They are just chatting there.

Then we are moving past them, Sera tugging me mostly toward the mansion.

The entrance is lofty and appears closed. "Are the doors locked? Are we too late?" I ask, my words coming out a bit too breathless.

A couple stands nearby. The woman catches my attention immediately as she's stunning, with long dark hair in a messy updo, loose tendrils trailing down her back. Her dress is the color of heather flowers, the low V-neck screaming sexy. She's paired it with stacked gold necklaces, and I notice beads and charms peeking through her updo. The man beside her is taller, equally striking. His brown hair is shorter but still has these perfect little curls at the ends. The white button-up he wears is open at the collar, paired with a suit jacket and a kilt.

The woman glances at the watch on his wrist. "It's 9:45 pm. We're early," she says, though I can hear music drifting from inside, the tempo building like the party is already in full swing.

I let out a sigh of relief. "Thank the gods."

The woman smiles at us. "I'm Tamsin, and this is Max."

I study them for a moment, grinning. "I'm Erynn. And this is my friend, Sera." My gaze drops to one of the necklaces around Tamsin's neck, recognizing the symbol. "You're from the House of Death and Diamond?"

The man, Max, nods. "We are."

"So, you've met the phantoms then?" Sera asks beside me.

I watch as Tamsin and Max exchange a look, some silent communication passing between them. Then Max gives us a lopsided smile and holds out his hand. My breath catches as his hand becomes translucent, almost ghost-like, before solidifying again moments later.

"That is cool!" I can't help but exclaim.

"It's a handy party trick," Max says modestly, turning back toward the double doors. "Shall we?" He holds his arm out to Tamsin, who stares at it with an expression I can't quite read. They seem to have some kind of staring contest before she gives him a bright smile that looks entirely artificial and hooks her arm through his. "We shall."

Max pushes open the doors with his free hand, and

despite their obvious weight, they swing open effortlessly. Sera and I follow them inside.

The transformation from the cool night air to the warm, perfumed atmosphere is immediate. Magic tingles against my skin as we step into a magnificent foyer.

The ceiling vaults so high it might as well be the sky, held up by columns that look carved from single pieces of white stone shot through with veins of gold. A chandelier that must weigh tons hangs from the center, crystals catching and throwing light in ways that create small rainbows on every surface.

The space feels mostly empty, as if everyone has already been drawn deeper into the mansion.

To our left, an older man in a black tuxedo with a crisp white shirt stands beside a pedestal. His face is deeply lined, and he wears a polite smile as he extends his hand expectantly.

I watch as Tamsin nudges Max with her arm, and he pulls out what looks like translucent invitations from his jacket pocket, handing them to the attendant.

"Welcome Mr. Fhearchair and Ms. Redthorne," the man says. "We have entertainment to the left, food to the right, and the bar is just up ahead." He gestures to each direction as he speaks.

Tamsin and Max exchange another glance, some unspoken question between them. Sera and I look at each other too, smiling.

"Can ye point us in the direction of the hostess? We would like to thank her for the invitation," Max says.

The attendant bows slightly. "She will find you, when the time is right."

Oh, mysterious, not that I'm surprised.

The attendant then turns to Sera and me, expecting our invitations. We step forward and we hand them over.

Once he lets us through, Sera gasps, and for once, I don't have a better response.

"This is either the best party ever, or we're about to become cautionary tales," I say.

"Both. Definitely both."

T hen we enter the ballroom, an enormous space Sera insists is two stories tall. Dim light bathes the room in front of us, and I'm awestruck.

People are dancing in a way that would have made my grandmother clutch her pearls. Bodies pressed super close together.

Every kind of supernatural must've been invited to the All Hallows' Eve Ball. I spot a guy with skin so pale it practically glows and is definitely giving vampire vibes. Another woman has eyes that flicker like candle flames when she laughs.

"Wow, this place is incredible," I murmur.

We turn to the bar first. There's a half-moon-shaped, white marble counter that seems to glow from within. Behind it, instead of shelves, bottles float in midair at various heights, rotating slowly, their contents shifting colors.

The bartender is almost impossibly beautiful, the kind of gorgeous that makes you aware of all your own flaws. His features are too perfect to be human, eyes that shift from green to gold to silver between blinks, movements that make pouring a drink look like a choreographed dance. He's wearing what might be a vest made of black scales, and his hair is as white as snow.

"Ladies," he says with a deep voice. "Welcome." Then he gestures to a menu that materializes on the bar's surface, written in golden script. "And what can I start you with?"

Sera and I lean in to read the options ranging from Moonlit Venom to Dragon's Breath to Phoenix Fire and so much more.

"Siren's Song sounds safe-ish?" I suggest.

"Safe is relative here," the bartender says. "But it's a good starter. Won't permanently alter your perception of reality."

"That's reassuring," Sera says dryly. "Two Siren's Songs, please."

He reaches for a bottle that definitely wasn't there

a second ago, pouring from a height that should splash everywhere but creates a perfect stream. The liquid is silver-white and literally glowing, leaving trails of light in the air. When the man slides the glasses over to us, frost spreads across the marble in their wake.

"To making terrible decisions in beautiful dresses," Sera says, lifting her glass.

"To not dying at our first fae party," I counter.

"That's the spirit. Low bars are easier to clear."

We clink glasses and drink. It tastes like... I don't have the words. Sweet and citrusy with a strength that lingers on my tongue with a hint of bubbles. Cold that burns down my throat but leaves warmth spreading through my chest and into my limbs.

"Oh," I breathe. "Oh, that's dangerous. I could drink five more."

"Right? I can feel my inhibitions dissolving. This is fantastic." Sera takes another sip. "I might actually tell Rich how I really feel tonight."

"You mean instead of just jumping him?"

"I can do both. I'm a multitasker."

"Speaking of Rich..." I start, but Sera's already gone rigid beside me, her grip on her glass tightening.

"Don't look behind us," she says.

So, naturally, I turn around.

Richard Voss is crossing the room toward us, and I hate him a little bit for how good he looks doing it. He moves through the crowd like a god, people stepping aside. Tall enough to tower over more, built like someone who kills professionally but makes it look easy. His hair is dark and a little too long. His eyes are nearly black.

He's wearing a tailored suit the color of midnight, because of course he is.

"He's coming this way," I whisper.

"I know," Sera whispers back. "Do I look okay? Is my lipstick smudged? Can you tell I've been thinking about him naked for two months?"

"Yes to all three, but in a good way."

"Hello, little witch." He stops directly in front of Sera, ignoring me completely, which is fine, because the intensity of his focus on her is making *me* blush.

"You absolute bastard," Sera breathes, but she's already leaning toward him. "Two fucking months without a word."

"I missed you too," he says softly, and then his hands are in her hair, her arms are around his neck, and they're kissing like the world is ending.

Not a polite "hello" kiss. Not even an "I've missed you" kiss. This is an "I'm going to devour you, and you're going to thank me for it" kiss. His hand fists in her elaborate updo, probably destroying hours of work. Her nails dig into his shoulders hard enough that I'm concerned for the suit. Someone behind us whistles. Someone else applauds.

They don't care.

When they finally come up for air, Sera's lipstick is somehow intact. Definitely magic.

"Erynn," she gasps without looking away from him, "I'm going to—"

"Go." I wave them off. "I'll be fine. Try not to destroy any furniture. This place looks expensive."

"No promises," Rich adds, and the look he gives her should come with a warning label. He nods at me once, the most acknowledgment I've ever gotten from him, then leads Sera away with a hand on her lower back that's somehow more intimate than the kiss.

"Have fun! Don't do anything I wouldn't do!" I call after them.

And then I'm alone at a bar in a fairy-tale mansion, surrounded by strangers in masks and shadows, holding a drink that tastes heavenly.

"Another?" the bartender asks, and there's sympathy in his shifting eyes.

"What's good for 'my best friend just abandoned me for her mysterious, probably assassin boyfriend and I haven't been to a party in years'?"

He considers this seriously, lips pinching to one side. "Phoenix Fire. Burns away the awkwardness, gives you confidence to mingle."

"Sold."

He pours something that's actually on fire. It's

beautiful and terrifying, gold and red swirling together in the glass.

"How do I…" I gesture at the flames.

"Just drink through them. They won't burn if you're meant to be here."

"And if I'm not meant to be here?"

"Then you have bigger problems than a flaming cocktail."

Fair point. I take a sip, flames licking at my nose. It tastes like cinnamon sugar. My spine straightens, my shoulders go back, and suddenly the dress doesn't feel too revealing.

"Better?" the bartender asks.

"Much." I grin, then finish the glass and set it on the counter.

I offer a grateful smile and turn toward the ballroom. Time to explore and see what a fae party has to offer.

The space is nothing like I imagined. I thought maybe chandeliers, some kind of magical elegance. But this is wild. Colors shimmer in the air like heat mirages. Music pulses from nowhere and everywhere. The energy is alive.

I linger at the edges, taking it all in. It's a lot, but not in a bad way.

A few spirits drift nearby, transparent, soft-edged, watching. They don't bother me. Most don't, unless I call to them. And often I don't even see them unless they're attached to someone.

But then something shifts.

The air thins, tightens. A slow, cold crawl slides along the back of my neck.

I turn just as he enters the ballroom.

Tall. Devastatingly handsome. Dark hair brushes just above his shoulders. His suit is immaculately cut, but it doesn't make him look polished. It makes him look dangerous. His jaw is clenched, mouth unsmiling, eyes scanning past everyone like the party is a distraction he'd rather not be part of.

People move around him. He doesn't try to blend in.

And before I can talk myself out of it, I step directly into his path.

He stops.

His gaze lifts to me. "Apologies," he murmurs, already shifting to move around me.

"You're looking for death... Oh, crap, sorry, that came out way more ominous than I meant." I laugh, tucking my hair behind my ear. "I get this vibe around you, like death is circling, looking for something. Sometimes the dead are so loud I forget to filter what comes out of my mouth. Occupational hazard." I smile and turn away, feeling dumb for blurting out such things. Most people don't appreciate it.

"I do seek death." His voice stops me.

I glance back. He's still watching me, but his gaze has dropped to my ears.

"You're fae," he says, eyes narrowing.

"Half fae, full-time ghost whisperer, part-time bad-decision maker," I say with a grin. "But in truth, I was gifted with a connection to the afterlife."

He hesitates. There's a flicker of something unreadable in his expression. Then—

"I'm hunting a pair of daggers. They are made of an ancient magic that predates this world, and they are deadly to anyone they encounter. Do you sense anything like that here?"

"Honestly? Parts of this place reek of death; many of these people have killed, and others are thinking about it." I stare at the crowd, rubbing my temple. "Your murder daggers could be right in front of me, and I'd probably miss them in all this supernatural noise. But hey, if they're that dangerous, I really hope you find them before someone decides to test them out at the party."

"Thank you," he murmurs, seeming unsatisfied but not being pushy.

I've never been great at tracking down lost objects... so I slip away.

I step a little farther into the room and immediately catch sight of something in the back corner. A crowd gathered around someone, laughing and gasping at whatever is happening.

So I make my way toward the crowd, curiosity pulling me forward.

But as I get closer, I can feel old magic, real, the kind that makes the air taste like copper and blood.

The woman at the center of the crowd is probably sixty, or possibly six hundred because with real magic, age becomes negotiable. Her silver hair is piled in an elaborate style held with pins that are definitely bones, tiny ones that might be from birds or something smaller. Her dress is midnight-blue velvet that doesn't reflect light so much as swallow it, and every finger bears a ring.

"Now then," the woman says, voice low and as rough as grave dirt. "Who among you remembers what Halloween really is? Not the parody that many peddle with candy and plastic bones—but the truth beneath the costume."

No one answers.

"Halloween," she says, "is not a celebration. It's a reckoning. The dead don't need an invitation tonight. They're already listening. Waiting. Watching. Because this is the hour when the rules weaken. The stories you forgot try to remember themselves. The things you buried dig back to the surface."

A sharp prickling spreads over my skin. I don't need the reminder; my awareness is already shifting. That buzzing at the edge of hearing, the pressure in the air that tells me the afterlife is closer than it should be.

She lifts a crimson apple from a basket full of them at her feet.

"Tonight, illusions rot. Fate demands payment in truth. If you dare ask her questions, she will answer."

Someone in the back speaks up. "Is this some kind of spell?"

Her eyes flash like something ancient waking. "Not a spell. A mirror. A test. A doorway, if you're foolish enough."

She produces a silver blade from her sleeve, impossibly small and wickedly sharp.

"You carve the peel in a single unbroken spiral. If it breaks, so does your tether to the answer. But if you succeed... and you cast it over your shoulder without looking... the first letter of your destined's name will appear with the way the peel lands."

"That's just folklore."

"Exactly," she replies. "And folklore is simply memory polished with time. Truth that learned how to lie."

Without breaking eye contact, she holds the apple and the blade like an offering.

"Who will ask fate to answer?"

A short man in a tux steps forward. Not bravado, more like something is dragging him by the spine. He slices, fumbles, throws. Gasps follow as the peel lands.

"An *S*," someone whispers.

The man's breath catches. "Sarah. My ex."

The old woman smiles slowly, as if she already knew. "Fate has no interest in your regrets. She plays the long game."

Then her eyes find me.

It's not a glance; it's a collision. I flinch before I can stop myself, every instinct screaming that something has noticed me that should not.

"You," she says, voice softer now. "You smell like the grave."

I don't respond.

"You walk too close to the edge," she continues. "One breath in this world, one borrowed from the next. I can hear them around you. Old ones. Hungry ones."

I feel them too.

The shift in temperature. The way the air thickens behind me, like the space I take up has grown crowded. I keep my posture neutral, but something just brushed my shoulder, and it wasn't alive.

"I speak to the dead," I say, more as a reminder to myself than a boast. "It's my job."

Her stare slices into me. Something inside me stirs in response. Not fear. Not exactly.

Recognition.

And deep down, I know I shouldn't have come tonight.

I catch movement in my peripheral vision. A translucent figure by the window, an elderly woman, Victorian dress, looking lost. Another by the door, a young man, modern clothes, bullet wound in his chest. They're always there if I look for them, especially on Halloween.

I carefully don't make eye contact with either ghost. Rule number one of being a medium: Don't acknowledge them unless you're ready to deal with them.

The woman smiles, slow and sharp. "Come, pretty girl. Take your turn."

She says it softly, but her voice carries low and is threaded with power, sliding into the bones of the room like a whispered command. Every head turns. The crowd shifts, attention locking on to me.

I hesitate. I hadn't planned to participate. Hadn't planned on being seen.

The woman tilts her head, eyes gleaming. "You, of all people, should know... fate doesn't wait for permission."

I glance around. No one else steps forward. They're watching me, not just with curiosity but with wariness. Recognition. I'm not one of them, not entirely, but they can feel the death I carry.

Something tightens in my chest, and I step forward.

I'm in front of her, then she presses an apple into my hand.

"Perfect," she croaks, as if this is the outcome she's been waiting for all along.

I take it.

"I don't really believe in fate," I say.

"Belief isn't required," she murmurs, just for me. "Only participation."

My hands move without waiting for my mind to catch up. The knife slides beneath the skin of the apple like it knows the path. Like it's done this before. Maybe it has. Maybe I have.

The peel unwinds in one perfect, gleaming coil.

The air in the room changes. Charged. Expectant.

The crowd has gone utterly silent. I can feel their attention crawling over me, slick and inescapable.

"Now," the woman says louder. "Don't think. Just throw."

I toss the peel over my shoulder.

A heartbeat later, there's a sound. Not an impact. Not a splash. Something deeper. A vibration. A growl that isn't human, isn't performative. It's real.

I turn.

The crowd behind me has already shifted again, clearing space around the source of the sound. And there he is.

The apple peel lies at his feet.

Tall. Broad. A man built like violence waiting for a reason. Hair dark and messy, framing a face too brutal to be pretty, too striking to be forgettable. Eyes like melted amber, and right now, they're glowing red at the edges, a silent warning.

He looks at the peel. Then at me.

A slow breath drags through his nose, and his jaw tenses.

There's a damp smear on his black jacket, darkened just enough to be noticeable. A thin sliver of apple and some tiny bits cling to the fabric. His shirt underneath is unbuttoned at the top, enough to show a slash of golden-brown skin and the edge of a tattoo curling up from beneath.

He wears tailored black slacks, clean, pressed, expensive. But there's something in the way he wears them that makes the elegance feel like an afterthought, like a cage he could tear off at any second.

And then, he bares his teeth.

Not a smile. A warning.

"Watch where you're throwing things," he growls.

"I didn't exactly aim," I say, but the words come out uneven.

He doesn't answer. Just turns, fury coiled tight in his shoulders, and walks away. People scramble to get out of his path.

"Charming," I mutter, more to fill the silence than anything.

The woman doesn't laugh. Instead, she watches him go with something like satisfaction.

"Oh, that one has lessons to learn," the woman murmurs, more to herself than to anyone else. Her eyes cut back to me like a blade slipping between ribs.

"Now, dear," she says. "Look at your peel."

I turn, heart hammering harder than I want to admit, and step to where it landed.

The shape the peel has taken has me tilting my head to the side. Curled just so, a perfect, elegant *C*.

Not a coincidence. Not an accident of gravity. Deliberate.

"She got a *C*," someone calls out.

But the woman has already turned her back. She's speaking to someone else, her shawl catching the candlelight as the crowd tightens around her once more.

Who was that guy?

Rude, sure. But honestly... if someone had chucked an apple peel at my brand-new dress, I'd probably growl too.

I rub my arms, trying to shake the chill.

Across the ballroom, I spot Sera.

She's laughing, twirling in Rich's arms, looking like the kind of carefree I haven't felt in years.

For a moment, I just watch her.
Then I square my shoulders.
No more weird magic games.
No more fate or tricks.
I came here to have fun... so damn it, I'm going to.

"*Vittu helvetti!!* Damn it!"

The Finnish curse rushes past my lips and ricochets off the bathroom walls with enough venom to strip paint. I'm scrubbing apple juice from my jacket.

"'Send Ash to find his mate,' they said. 'The stars have spoken,' they said. Well, the stars can take their prophecies and shove them up their asses. I knew I shouldn't have attended. I have too much to do back home with the pack, and you sure as fuck can't rush finding your mate."

Every surface around me gleams with the kind of perfection that only magic can maintain. Gold fixtures that never tarnish, mirrors framed in silver so pure it sets my nerves and wolf on edge. We're not weak to silver in the way some may think, but pure silver still makes my skin crawl, some ancestral memory of when it could actually hurt us.

Koi fish swim eternal circles on the tiles, scales shifting between copper and gold and colors that shouldn't exist. Seaweed painted in the corners sways in an invisible current, reaching up toward a ceiling painted to look like the surface of water seen from below, complete with filtered sunlight.

Tentacles—because apparently someone decided this bathroom needed tentacles—curl around the base of the sink and up the sides of the stalls. They're carved from what might be obsidian or maybe something else entirely.

The chandelier overhead shouldn't exist. It's made from what appear to be water droplets, each one catching and throwing light in ways that create rippling shadows across every surface.

"Thirty-two years," I inform the swordfish mounted on the far wall, wringing out my jacket. "I've survived without a mate this far. Would another decade kill them? Suddenly the pack needs their Alpha paired off."

Nine months. That's how long my father has been dead. And it's been fucking bliss being out from under his shadow, his constant criticism, his iron-fisted control over every aspect of pack life. The bastard clung to life through pure spite, too mean to die even when his organs started shutting down one by one. The pack celebrated for three days straight when he finally stopped breathing. Bonfires and drinking and dancing because the tyrant was finally gone.

I didn't celebrate. I stood over his grave in the rain, waiting to feel something. Relief, satisfaction, maybe even grief. Instead, I felt nothing. Just the weight of becoming everything he said I could never be, inheriting a pack held together by fear rather than loyalty.

Now the elders want me mated. Want the bloodline secured. Want little Alpha babies running around to ensure the pack's future. As if I don't have enough problems trying to rebuild what my father destroyed, trying to earn trust instead of demanding obedience through violence.

Movement catches my eye. The swordfish's tail fin twitches.

I freeze, watching. The fin goes still. My imagination, obviously. Too much fae magic in the air making me see things that aren't there. I turn back to the sink, running more water over my jacket.

The swordfish gasps.

Not a small movement, not a trick of the light. A full-body shudder that sends cracks spreading through the mounting plaque like lightning through glass. The wood splinters, screws ripping free from the wall with sounds like tiny gunshots. The preserved fish—the very dead, very stuffed fish—tears free from its mount and hits the marble floor with a wet slap that echoes off every surface.

For a moment, I just stare at it. Then, with the kind of calm that comes from having seen too much weird shit to be properly surprised anymore, I walk over and crouch beside the supposedly deceased fish.

It's flopping. Not just twitching, but full-on thrashing, tail slapping against the marble hard enough to crack the tiles. Gills desperately trying to pull in water that isn't there. The glass eye is rolling wildly in its socket before fixing on me with an expression I can only describe as pissed off. The fish's mouth opens and closes, and I swear I can hear it trying to scream.

"You're supposed to be dead," I tell it conversationally, maintaining eye contact because looking away from a resurrected swordfish feels like admitting defeat.

The fish's response is to thrash harder, its sword scraping against the marble.

"Whatever magic runs this house, I want no part of it. You hearing me, fish? This is your problem now."

The temperature drops so fast that my next breath comes out as fog. Frost spreads across the mirrors in fractals that look almost like writing in a language I don't recognize. The chandelier overhead dims, its water droplets freezing solid with tiny cracking sounds.

That's when Mikael walks through the wall.

My heart doesn't just skip; it stops entirely, a full second of absolute stillness before slamming back to life hard enough that I'm surprised my ribs don't crack.

"Fuck no." The word comes out strangled, barely recognizable as human speech. "No, no, no. Not possible. Not fucking possible. You're dead."

Mikael stands there in the battle gear he died in, and the detail is horrifying in its perfection. Black vest torn open at the chest, revealing not just the wounds that killed him but also the damage beneath—broken ribs visible through ghostly flesh, one lung collapsed, the strange angle of his shoulder where it had been dislocated in the fight. Three claw marks run from his throat to his stomach, so deep that, in life, you could see his spine through the gore.

The memory hits with the force of a sledgehammer to the chest...

Rain turning the battlefield into a swamp of mud and blood. The warehouse district, abandoned since the last surge, now crawling with Bruck pack members who'd taken a local pack's children. Forty-three of them, all under sixteen, stolen from their beds while we'd been dealing with a territory dispute up north.

Twenty of us against twice that many. Not good odds, but the ferals that make up the Bruck pack are usually disorganized, fighting each other as much as their enemies. These ones were different. Coordinated. Led by Cain and his younger brother, Tobias. Their father rules the wild pack, but he's too old now and lets his sons make the calls.

Mikael on my left, and his twin, Magnus, on my right. The plan was simple. Hold the bridge while our strike team extracted the children.

The first wave hit like a tsunami of teeth and claws. Bodies everywhere, the screaming of children mixing with howls of rage and pain. I was fighting three at once when I heard Mikael's roar cut short. Turned to see him separated from the line, surrounded by six ferals who'd clearly targeted him specifically.

"Ash!" His voice, desperate. "Ash, help!"

But if I left the line, if I abandoned the bridge, the ferals would flood through. The strike team would be trapped. More would die.

"Hold the line!" I roared, even as I watched them tear into him. Even as he screamed my name with his last breath. Even as Magnus begged me to save his brother, tears mixing with rain and blood on his face.

All the children were saved. Seven warriors lost. Mikael died calling for me, and I let him, because that's what Alphas do. We make the hard choices. We sacrifice the few for the many.

We live with the ghosts.

"Ash?" Mikael's voice sounds wrong, echoing from somewhere deeper than his throat, maybe deeper than this reality. "You look rough, brother. Rougher than me, and I'm dead."

My hands shake as I press back against the wall, the cold tile shocking against my palms but not as shocking as my dead packmate standing there making jokes. "You're dead. I carried your body myself. Buried you next to your mother. You're dead."

He tilts his head, a gesture so perfectly Mikael that my chest aches. "Death is negotiable in places of power, brother. You know this. Or did you skip that part of the lore lessons to chase girls?"

"I've never seen ghosts. Never. That's not my gift, not my burden." My voice cracks on the last word.

"Maybe it is now." He steps closer, and I can smell him—copper, rain, and... death, maybe. Or regret. "Speaking of family, how's Marina holding up?"

"What?" The question is so normal, so casual, that it breaks my brain a little. "Your sister? She's... she's managing. The pack provides for her."

"Good, good." He nods, then his expression shifts to something more serious. "Tell her that new lover of hers is stealing from her. Going through Mother's jewelry, the stuff she kept hidden in the floorboards."

"Marina doesn't have a—what are you talking about?" My mind races, trying to process this. "How do you know about any jewelry? How are you *here*?"

Mikael shrugs, a gesture made surreal by the way his damaged shoulder doesn't quite move right.

"Death makes you notice things. See patterns. Like how you're panicking right now instead of thinking. Very unlike you, Alpha."

The title hits wrong coming from him. He never called me "Alpha" when alive, just "Ash" or, when being particularly annoying, "Your Royal Wolfness."

The bathroom door slams against the wall as I barrel through it, desperate to escape my dead pack-mate who won't stop talking. I need air, space, something that makes sense.

I crash directly into someone coming around the corner at speed.

The bump sends them flying backward, and instinct kicks in before thought. My arms wrap around a slim waist, yanking them against me to prevent them from hitting the floor. The momentum spins us, my back hitting the wall as I absorb the impact, keeping them safe even as my spine protests the collision.

Soft. That's the first thought. Soft and warm and curves that fit against me perfectly. She barely reaches my chin, forcing me to look down at platinum blonde hair that glints in the hallway light. Her body is pressed along mine from chest to thigh, and I can feel every breath she takes, quick little gasps that move her breasts against my chest in deeply distracting ways.

"Are you okay?" My voice comes out rougher than intended.

She looks up, and everything else ceases to exist.

Striking green eyes that hold entire winters—not cold but fierce, beautiful in the way avalanches are beautiful, deadly and inevitable. Her face is all sharp but softened by full lips painted dark red. An expression that says she's trouble in the best and worst ways.

But it's her scent that nearly drops me. Vanilla and lightning. How lightning has a scent, I don't know, but it does—ozone and electricity and power. Beneath that, honey, a sweetness that has me salivating. It's contradictory and impossible and absolutely intoxicating.

We stay frozen, her palms splayed across my chest, my hands spanning her waist, bodies molded together. I can feel her heartbeat, rapid and strong. Can feel the heat of her through the fabric of her dress. Can feel the moment she realizes our position and decides not to move away.

"I-it's you. I'm so sorry about the apple peel earlier," she finally says. "I didn't mean—"

"To mark your territory?" The words slip out before I can stop them, my brain apparently deciding that flirting is the appropriate response to this situation. "Interesting technique. Most shifters just use teeth. More traditional. Less sticky."

Her eyes flash, leaving me grinning. "If I wanted to mark you, I'd be much more creative than apple warfare."

"That seemed more like a crime of opportunity."

Her fingers flex against my chest, nails pressing slightly through the fabric, and there's something predatory in the gesture that calls to the Alpha in me. "Maybe you were exactly where I wanted you."

"Covered in apple juice in a bathroom with a resurrected fish?"

She blinks, momentarily thrown. "What?"

"Fae party madness. Don't ask." I should let her go. I should step back. Instead, my thumb traces her waist, feeling the heat of her skin through silk. "You smell incredible."

The words hang between us, too honest, too raw, stripping away the banter and leaving something hungry and dangerous. Her pupils dilate, black swallowing green, and then she leans in and presses her nose against my chest, inhaling deeply.

Not a subtle sniff. Not trying to hide it. Full-on breathing me in with the kind of focus usually reserved for wolf identifying. I feel the exhale against my shirt, warm and damp, and my control slips several crucial notches.

"So do you," she murmurs against my chest, and the vibration of her words goes straight through me. Another inhale, longer, her whole body pressing closer. "God, what is that? I want to eat it."

"That's an interesting way to describe a scent."

She pulls back just enough to glance up at me, but

not enough to actually create distance. We're still pressed together in ways that would be considered foreplay in some cultures. "Seriously, what cologne is this? It's intoxicating."

"I don't wear any."

"Sure you don't." Her nose wrinkles adorably, and then she's leaning in again, this time toward my neck, and I have to lock my knees to stay upright. "Nobody naturally smells this delicious."

I can't help but laugh.

"Pine," she says, but her face flushes. "I think it's, like, pine. And musk. And something sexy too..." She trails off, genuinely blushing. "Something that makes me want to do inappropriate things."

"Such as?"

"Such as continuing to sniff a complete stranger."

"I'm not judging. You smell like you'd taste like electricity and wild woods."

"That's not a thing."

"You're making it a thing."

She laughs, this throaty sound that has my cock throbbing. "Do you practice lines like that, or do they just come to you in the moment?"

"This is not practiced." I mean it. Nothing in my experience has prepared me for a woman who crashes into me, smells like heaven and danger, and apparently wants to inhale me like a drug. "I'm Ash, by the way."

"Erynn." She tries to step back, but her heel catches on the uneven rug. She pitches forward, hands shooting out for balance.

Her nails rake across my forearm as she tries to steady herself, and pain flares sharp and unexpected. Not normal pain, but the burning lines of actual wounds. I hiss, more from surprise than hurt, and look down to see torn fabric and blood welling from four perfect scratches.

"Shit!" She jerks back, staring at her hands in horror.

Her nails have become claws. Not the painted nails from moments ago, but actual claws that are pristine white, curved, at least an inch long, and sharp enough to part flesh without effort. They gleam under the hallway lights, beautiful and terrible.

"I did that?" Her voice pitches higher, panic threading through it as she stares at my arm. "Oh, shit. Oh, shit, my hands, what's wrong with them?"

She holds them up, fingers spread, staring at the claws with revulsion and terror. They're not retracting, not shifting back to normal. Just remaining there, permanent, and she's looking at them with the expression of someone who's discovered they've grown extra limbs.

"You've never shifted before?" I ask carefully, watching her face pale to the point where I'm concerned she might faint.

"Shifted?" The word comes out as almost a shriek. "I don't transform. I'm not a shifter. I don't turn into... into... whatever this is!"

"But I assumed by your scent and your ears that you were mixed blood, shifter and fae." They're slightly pointed, barely noticeable unless you're looking, but definitely there.

"No." She shakes her head violently, platinum hair flying. "No shifter blood. My grandmother was fae, but of mixed heritage. Some siren, some earth fae, maybe a touch of banshee, which would explain the death stuff, but not shifter. Never shifter. We don't have shifters in my family. We have alcoholics and mediums and the occasional pyromaniac."

Behind her, through the wall, Mikael reappears. He seems more solid this time, details sharper—the freckles across his nose, the way his left eye was always slightly greener than the right.

"She's not lying," Mikael observes, circling us with interest. "But she's not entirely right either. Something's different about her. Wrong. She smells like wolf, but not wolf. Death, but not dead. Yours, but not yours."

"Not now, Mikael," I mutter without thinking.

"Who's Mikael?" Erynn asks, looking around with those too-green eyes.

Shit. She'll think I'm crazy. "Nobody. Just... thinking out loud. Bad habit."

Mikael grins, and it's the same shit-eating grin that got us into so much trouble as teenagers. "Nobody? I'm hurt, brother. Here I thought we had something special. Remember when you cried because Sean ate your last piece of birthday cake? You were fifteen. It was adorable."

"I was not fifteen, but eight," I snap, then realize I'm arguing with a ghost.

"Eight what?" Erynn asks, clearly confused.

"Nothing. Different conversation. In my head. Which I'm having. Apparently."

Mikael walks straight through her, and she shivers violently, wrapping her arms around herself. "Okay, that was weird. Did you feel that? Like someone walked over my grave. Or through me. Can someone walk through me? Is that a thing that happens at fae parties?"

"You felt that?" I stare at Mikael, who looks equally surprised.

"The sudden cold? Yes." She looks around again, then directly at where Mikael stands, though her eyes don't focus on him. "There's something here. I can feel it. But I can't see it, which never happens. I see dead people for a living. It's literally on my business cards."

"You put 'I see dead people' on your business cards?" I ask, desperate to deflect.

"Well, no. It says 'Spiritual Medium and Afterlife

Consultant.' But the point stands. I should be able to see whatever's making you talk to yourself."

"Tell her about the wet dog incident," Mikael suggests. "Women love vulnerable men, and I think she likes you."

I ignore him.

Someone stumbles down the hallway, drunk and laughing, reeking of fairy wine. They bump into Erynn hard enough to send her reeling forward again. This time when I catch her, something's different. Her body temperature is spiking, skin feverish through her dress.

"Something's wrong," she gasps, doubling over. One hand clutches her stomach, and the other braces against my chest. "It's moving. Inside me. There's something inside me trying to get out."

Her claws extend further, and the sound that comes out of her is a whimper that becomes a growl that grows into something else entirely.

"Tell me exactly what you feel," I demand, keeping my voice steady despite my own growing panic. Something is happening here beyond normal fae-party weirdness.

"Hungry," she whispers, and her voice has changed, rougher, deeper. "So hungry, but not for food. For... running. Hunting. I want to chase something. I want to catch it. I want to—" She looks up at me with terror-filled eyes. "The spirits warned me not to come tonight."

"She needs to shift," Mikael says, all humor gone from his voice.

Yet she insists she's not a shifter. I reach for my wolf, the constant companion that's been with me since my first change as a child. The presence that defines me, grounds me, makes me what I am.

Nothing.

The space where my wolf lives is empty. Not sleeping, not distant, not angry. Fucking gone. A void where half my soul should be. Cold dread floods me.

"I need air," Erynn gasps, then bolts.

She moves wrong, too fast for a fae, too clumsy for a shifter, too desperate for anything controlled.

I watch her disappear through the ballroom doors, every instinct screaming at me to follow. Not to help. To hunt.

"Well, go after her, lover boy," Mikael says quietly. "Unless you want to explain to the elders how you let your mate get torn apart by your own wolf."

"She's not my—" I stop. The apple. The witch with her knowing smile. The peel hitting me, most likely marking me. And now with the full moon outside, she's transforming...

"The spirits warned her," I say aloud, pieces clicking together with horrible clarity. "They knew this would happen."

"Spirits usually do. Cryptic bastards, the lot of them." Mikael starts fading, becoming translucent. "Better hurry. Your wolf's not known for its patience, and her body's not built for what it wants to do."

It all comes at me quickly—my ability to see ghosts, her shifting into a wolf even though she isn't one.

We'd been cursed, and somehow our abilities swapped. How the fuck does that happen?

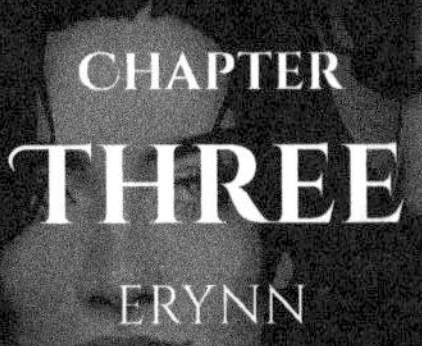

THREE

Something is trying to claw its way out of my skin.

"Okay, universe," I gasp, stumbling deeper into the woods behind the mansion, my heels long abandoned somewhere between the ballroom and here. "I get it. I shouldn't have mocked that fortune teller last month. Or laughed at that tarot reading. Or called astrology 'space racism.' I'm sorry, okay? Please stop turning me inside out!"

My bones feel wrong. Not broken, but rearranging, like someone is playing games with my skeleton and forgot to read the rules. Each step sends waves of sharpness through my body, my joints bending in directions that shouldn't exist, muscles pulling against anchor points that keep shifting. The beautiful blue dress I borrowed from Sera is already torn at the seams, and I hear more rips forming with every convulsion.

The trees around me aren't helping my panic. They're too tall, too twisted, shadows falling in directions that don't match the moon overhead. The bark has patterns that might be natural whorls or might be faces, watching me stumble.

"This is fine," I tell myself, then immediately laugh because it comes out as half groan, half hysteria. "Everything is fine. You're just having a supernatural breakdown at a party full of creatures that could kill you. Except, nothing about this is standard. And I'm talking to myself in the spooky forest."

My hands—claws, they're fucking claws now—dig into a tree trunk for support. The bark splits like paper, leaving deep gouges that immediately start weeping sap that glows faintly green. Because of course it does. Can't even have normal tree damage in this place.

"I'm sorry, tree," I whisper, watching the luminous sap drip.

My spine ripples, and I cry out in agonizing pain. I drop to my knees, claws digging into the ground, and the heavy soil scent floods me. Earth and decay and growing things. Something died here days ago—a rabbit, my new senses inform me, taken by an owl. There's water running underground, twenty feet down, mineral-rich and cold. The moss on the north side of the trees is actually a slightly different species from the moss on the south side, and I know this because they smell different.

"Stop it," I beg my own body. "Please stop knowing things I shouldn't know."

A branch snaps behind me.

Something is approaching. My head whips around so fast my neck protests, vertebrae cracking in complaint, and every muscle in my body locks into a tension I've never felt before.

My heartbeat is so loud it should be echoing off the trees. But from somewhere in my chest comes a growl.

Wait, I don't growl... I make sarcastic comments and avoid confrontation and sometimes squeak when startled, but I definitely don't produce sounds that belong to apex predators.

There's a shadow between the trees way behind me. Human-shaped but moving wrong, too fluid, too purposeful. Not stumbling like someone lost, not hurrying like someone scared. Moving like something that knows exactly where its prey is and has all the time in the world to collect it.

"Nope," I breathe, and the word comes out with a rumble that vibrates through my chest. "Nope, nope, nope."

Fight or flight. My brain screams to run, but something in me battles to face the danger. Except this isn't my land to protect. I don't have property. I have a small place with a concerning amount of dead plants and a ghost cat that isn't mine but won't leave.

Flight wins.

I run.

Not normal running. Not even panicked human running. Something else takes over, my body dropping lower, using my claws for balance and propulsion. Muscles I didn't know existed fire away, turning me into something built for speed and survival. The dress gives up entirely, shredding around me in confetti that catches on branches.

The woods blur past, but my vision is different too. Clearer in the darkness, noticing movement in peripheral spaces, processing information faster than my human brain can interpret. An owl takes flight thirty feet to my left. Something small scurries up a tree trunk to my right.

My chest burns with more than exertion, with fury that I'm being hunted, with terror of what's going on with me. The growl that escapes me this time is mine, fully mine.

I check behind me and spot the shadow farther away but not giving up.

"Stop following me!" I shout over my shoulder, but it comes out garbled, half-human words mixed with sounds that belong to something with too many teeth.

I push harder, feet—paws—barely touching the ground. Wait... What the fuck? I stumble, nearly losing my momentum. White fur runs up my front legs, because I'm now an animal. A fucking wolf! My heart races as panic rises, clawing at my chest. I don't know how this happened. I don't know what's happening to me.

My limbs are too fast, too wild, and every step moves with a strength that doesn't feel like mine. The forest seems to open for me, or maybe I'm finally seeing the paths that were always there, concealed from normal eyes.

My left paw catches on a root, hidden under deceptive leaves. The world tilts, spins, and I'm rolling. I come up in a crouch, facing my pursuer, lips peeled back to show teeth eager to bite.

Ash bursts through the underbrush and is on me in seconds.

His weight slams into me, sending us both to the ground in a tangle of limbs.

I'm pinned beneath him, his body covering mine completely. We're both breathing hard, and this close, I stare into the wildness behind his eyes. Pine needles stick in my hair, the earth cold against my back, and I'm hyperaware of every point where our bodies touch.

He lowers his head, lips near my ear. "Stand down." His voice is low and firm.

A breath gushes past my lips. Then again, sharper.

"Easy," he murmurs. "She's not prey. She's mine." Is he talking to the wolf?

A tremor rolls through me.

I blink at him, stunned.

A sudden pull, deep and instinctive, like a thread being yanked tight, pulses through me. My muscles seize. My breath stutters.

In a heartbeat, the world tilts. A rush like falling and flying at the same time roars through my veins, and then everything is twisted. My bones crack. Heat floods my skin. My paws are hands. My chest heaves.

My breath catches. Muscles lock. And slamming me back into my human body.

I'm gasping on my back, skin bare, chest rising too fast, too exposed beneath him, the cold sinking in like a blade.

His weight remains over me. His hands grip my wrists, and the heat of his body is a brand against my naked skin.

I freeze.

His gaze drags over me, slow and intense, then meets my eyes. "Welcome back, pretty girl," he murmurs.

My breath stutters. "Why the hell were you chasing me like a lunatic?" I snarl, and wow, I can actually snarl now. It comes from somewhere deep in my chest, reverberating through both our bodies. "I'm dying out here, and you're playing predator?"

"I was trying to find you, not—" His explanation cuts off as a howl rips from my throat. Not a human imitation of a wolf, not the kind of sound drunk people make at the moon. The real thing, powerful enough to echo through the trees, to announce to every creature in hearing distance that something wild is here. It's beautiful and terrifying and completely involuntary.

We both freeze, staring at each other. His weight shifts, and I can sense the thump of his heartbeat against my chest, quick but steady.

"Did I just—"

"Yes."

"That came from me?"

"Yes."

"I howled. I actually howled. Like a wolf."

"Yes."

"Stop saying yes!"

"No."

Despite the claws, the supernatural crisis, the fact that I'm partially pinned under a relative stranger in a dark forest, I laugh. Or try to. It comes out as something between a giggle and a yip, which is somehow worse than the howl.

"This isn't happening," I babble, because talking is better than thinking about how real this is, how his scent is everywhere now, overwhelming my senses. How I'm damn naked with my dress shredded through the woods. "I'm having a stroke. Or someone spiked the fairy wine with hallucinogens. Or I'm still in bed and this is the world's most elaborate stress dream."

"This is no dream." His weight shifts slightly. "Right now, we need to talk about what's happening to you." His thumb brushes against my skin, but it sends sparks through my entire body.

"What's happening to me is that I think I must be cursed and someone really hates me," I pant, trying to ignore how good he smells this close. "I told you, I'm not a shifter. This shouldn't be possible."

"I know," he murmurs. His weight is still over me. "I think we're connected. That witch in the mansion, the apple peel... she did something to us."

"That was just a party trick—" But the words barely leave my mouth before something inside me twists hard, like it's pushing back.

A sudden pressure builds in my chest. The wolf thrashes like it's clawing for the surface, no longer content to wait. My breath catches. Heat pulses beneath my skin. My heartbeat stumbles.

I scream out, and Ash instantly rolls off me.

Then my body arches without warning, spine bowing. The change is violent and undeniable. I should be terrified by the sound of my bones breaking and re-forming, but the thing inside me is singing with freedom once more.

The world explodes into sensation like the first change.

Ash's scent dominates, but beneath that, I pick up the deer that passed not long ago. Colors fade but contrast sharpens. Every leaf, every shadow, every tiny movement becomes crisper. The night isn't dark anymore; it's graduated shades of silver and gray that show more detail than human daylight.

I push myself onto my side, scrambling onto all fours again.

Panic floods through me because I have zero control.

Is this how it feels for shifters? The thought is mine but echoes strangely, bouncing off this new presence that seems amused by my confusion.

I sniff the air, and Ash's scent has me salivating. Which should be concerning but mostly just makes me want to get closer, to rub against him, to mark him with my scent so everyone knows—

What the hell am I thinking?

I prowl forward, lips peeling back to show teeth. My reflection glints in his eyes, and I see myself for a moment—huge white wolf, bigger than any natural wolf has a right to be, eyes glowing gold in the darkness.

"Easy," Ash says, voice dropping into something commanding that makes my spine tingle. "Now, back off."

My legs lock, refusing to move forward despite

every instinct screaming at me to pounce. I push against the compulsion.

"Sit," he demands in that same tone, and my ass hits the ground before I can process the command. What the hell?

"Roll over." He grins, enjoying himself.

I'm on my back, paws in the air, belly exposed, before the fury washes over me. The position is submissive, vulnerable, everything the wolf in my head hates. How dare he? I'm not a dog doing tricks for treats. I'm not his pet to command.

The wolf agrees, insulted by the casual dominance, by the assumption that we'll just obey because he has a nice voice and authority issues.

I scramble onto my feet, tail stiff behind me. My ears flatten as I start to circle him slowly, deliberately, each paw-step silent against the forest floor. The wolf wants blood. Or at least pride. Maybe both.

Ash watches me, brow lifted like this is all very amusing. "Okay. Take it slow. Sit."

I bare my teeth.

"Stay?"

A warning growl rumbles in my throat.

His smirk twitches. "Play dead?"

I lunge a step closer, lips peeled back over fangs, and that's when something shifts in his gaze. The amusement drains, replaced by focus. He takes a step back. Then another.

"All right," he mutters. "Message received."

Too late.

I surge forward, claws outstretched. He dodges fast, but not fast enough. My claws catch his shirt, ripping fabric as he spins away and bolts into the woods.

"This is not how this is supposed to work!" he shouts, vaulting over a fallen log with impressive grace.

I chase because the thing inside me loves to hunt, lives for it, was born for it.

Ash is fast, dodging trees with inches to spare, sliding under low branches. But I'm faster now, four legs better than two.

"Stay back!" he shouts, that commanding tone again. "Stop!"

The compulsion flares over me like a wave, trying to freeze my muscles, to force obedience. But I push through it, drawing on every ounce of stubbornness that's ever made me argue with ghosts who insisted they weren't dead. The wolf lends its strength.

Ash breaks into a clearing lit by moonlight, and I spot my chance. I launch myself at him, all four paws leaving the ground, body stretched to its full length. We collide in midair, his attempt to dodge coming a fraction too late.

We hit the ground hard, rolling twice before

coming to a stop with me on top, paws on his chest, teeth at his throat.

My jaws part, teeth resting against his skin. Not breaking it, not yet, but holding. A growl rumbles from somewhere deep in my chest, vibrating through both of us. This close, his scent is overwhelming. A combination of fear, sweat, arousal, and challenge all mixed together.

He goes perfectly still beneath me.

He should be terrified. Any sane person would be scared with a wolf's teeth at their throat. But his heartbeat, while fast, isn't panicked. His scent carries adrenaline but also... arousal? Trust? That can't be right.

"You going to bite me, or are we just going to stay like this?" His voice is steady, conversational, as though we're discussing the weather instead of the fact that I could tear his throat out with one flex of my jaw.

I inhale deeply, trying to understand this man who isn't afraid of me even when he should be.

He's special. Important. *Mine*, the wolf whispers, or maybe I do.

Slowly, carefully, I ease the pressure of my teeth. My tongue flicks out without permission, tasting the salt of his skin and... the copper tang of blood? There, on his arm, those scratches from earlier when my claws first emerged. They're already healing, but I clean them anyway, an instinct I don't understand but can't resist. The blood tastes like electricity on my tongue, sending sparks through my entire body.

I move back to his neck where my teeth had been, licking the small indentations, and he makes a sound that's part groan, part growl.

"Shift back," he states in that deep and rough voice that I find too irresistible. "Now, Erynn. Come back to me."

It feels like thunder under my skin, power grabbing hold of my bones and pulling. The wolf beside me in my mind protests, receding reluctantly but unable to resist whatever authority his voice carries. The change hurts more, my body protesting the return to a form that suddenly feels too small, too limiting, too human.

When it's over, I'm straddling him, completely naked, shaking from the transformation.

The moonlight does unfair things to his features, sharpening already dangerous cheekbones, making his amber eyes glow with their own light. His dark hair is mussed from our chase, strands falling across his forehead. There's a wildness to him that calls to whatever is now living inside me, and the smile spreading across his face is pure sin.

"Good to have you back," he almost purrs, which has me shuddering with a strange excitement. "Enjoy your first hunt?"

"I—" Words are hard when he's looking at me like that, like I'm something magnificent instead of a naked disaster straddling him in the woods. "That was—"

But my emotions take control, and suddenly, I'm leaning down and kissing him.

It's a mistake. I know it immediately. Because the moment our lips meet, I can't stop. The kiss isn't gentle. It's hungry, desperate, filled with the wild energy still coursing through my veins. His hands come up to tangle in my hair, holding me close, and when he nips at my bottom lip, I moan.

He rolls us, pine needles and earth soft beneath my back, his weight pressing me down. I should feel trapped, but I don't. If anything, I'm grounded, kept from floating away on this tide of impossible sensation. He kisses like he's trying to devour me, and the wolf inside me purrs its approval.

I try to flip us back, to take control, but his hand catches my wrists, pinning them above my head.

"So that's how this is?" I gasp against his mouth, testing his grip just to determine how easily he holds me.

"Problem?" His teeth find my pulse point, and I arch beneath him, a whimper escaping that I'll deny later.

"I don't submit."

"You did earlier. Sat so pretty when I told you to."

His free hand traces down my side, leaving trails of fire in its wake.

"That was different. That was—" I lose my train of thought as he does something with his tongue on my neck that shorts out my brain. "Not fair. Nothing about this is fair."

He pulls back off me just enough to look at me, and with the heat in his eyes, I'm squirming. "Give me a moment."

The loss of his warmth leaves me whimpering. But he's only gone for a second, shrugging off his jacket. It's thick and oversized, and he lays it out on the ground beside us.

"Come here," he states, patting the makeshift blanket. It's not quite a command, but there's something in his voice that has me moving before I even think to resist.

I crawl to the makeshift blanket, hyperaware of his eyes tracking my naked body. "You're playing with fire," I warn him as he unbuttons his shirt and takes it off, laying it on the ground for more coverage. Then he moves to join me.

"Maybe I like the burn." His hand cups my face, thumb tracing my cheekbone with unexpected gentleness. "And you're shaking."

"I just turned into a wolf. I think I'm entitled to some trembling."

"Fair point." He pulls me against him, both of us

on our knees. The skin-to-skin contact makes us inhale sharply. "Better?"

The moonlight catches the sweat on his skin, highlighting every line of muscle. The wolf in my head is pushing me toward something primal and dangerous.

"This isn't like me at all," I whisper. "I don't do this... I've never..."

"Yet you can't keep your hands off me," he teases. His fingers trace my jaw, tilting my face up to meet his gaze. "The wolf thinks you belong to me."

His admission empties my mind of thought or a response.

"And the wolf wants me to devour you," I tease.

"Then devour me." He shifts, rising to his feet, hands moving to his belt. The sound of leather sliding through loops is impossibly loud in the quiet forest. "Show me that hunger you're fighting so hard to control."

My breath catches as he towers over me where I kneel. The power dynamic changes as I glance up at him.

One hand tangles in my hair, not pulling, just holding. "Scared?"

"Excited," I correct, and my voice comes out breathy, nothing like my usual sarcasm. "The wolf... she wants things. Dark things. Things I've never wanted before."

"Tell me." His thumb traces my bottom lip, and I

catch it between my teeth, biting gently. His breath hitches. "Tell me what you want."

"To taste you," I whisper. "To mark you. To make you lose that perfect control you're holding on to so tightly."

He laughs, low and dangerous. "You think I'm in control right now?"

"Aren't you always?"

"No." His hand tightens in my hair, and I gasp at the sensation. "Not with you. Never with you. You undo me, Erynn. Make me want things I shouldn't want."

"Like what?"

"Like keeping you here, on your knees, looking at me like I'm something you want to consume." His voice drops to a growl that makes the wolf in my head purr. "Like letting you..."

My heart stutters, and for a beat, I just kneel there, stunned by how badly I want him. Since when am I this girl? The kind who drops to her knees, breathless, begging, unhinged?

Apparently... since now.

Because I reach for him, fingers fumbling at the waistband of his pants. My hands are shaking from this need, wild and hungry and spiraling fast. I can't stop touching him. I don't want to stop.

He's still standing over me, solid and massive and

watching me like he's trying not to lose his head. My hands yank at the zipper.

"I want all of you," I breathe. "And I don't want you in control. I want you wrecked."

Who is this girl I've become?

My knees press into the ground as I stare up at him, the air thick with heat. There's a war inside me. The part that seeks control and the one losing the battle for something darker. Wilder. Hungrier.

And Ash knows it.

He crouches beside me again, so close I can feel the warmth coming off him, and his mouth brushes my ear. "You want to be in control? Then don't beg. Don't tremble. Don't look at me like I'm the only thing keeping you from coming undone. Show me your teeth, little wolf. Bite, scratch, take. Or—"

His fingers curl around my chin, forcing me to meet his eyes.

"Submit."

The word cleaves me in half.

As he rises again, I breathe raggedly, watching him undo the button of his pants. I don't think. I just move. I tug the fabric down, and his cock springs free. It's thick, flushed, heavy with want, and I'm clenching my thighs with desperation.

My breath stutters. I blink once, twice. There's no preparing for the sight of him. He's large.

"Show me how much you need me," he states, gaze heavy-lidded and full of fire.

I stare up at him through my lashes, defiant. "Oh, you think I won't?"

I don't even recognize the voice coming out of me. This isn't who I was before. But then again, I wasn't a wolf before either. I was never on my knees, mouth watering, body slick and trembling with need. He's dragged something primal out of me, something raw and ravenous.

I purr, lips brushing the base of his shaft. "I'm going fuck your cock with my mouth."

His fingers shudder as they slide into my hair.

I drag my tongue along the underside of his shaft, watching his eyes flutter closed and his jaw clench. I slide my lips over his tip, taking my time to press my mouth down his shaft. I claim him, slow but certain, tongue curling as I sink deeper, loving the way he shudders, the way all that Alpha dominance fractures at my touch.

"Fuck," he breathes, hands hanging limp at his sides.

I pull back just far enough to speak, licking my lips. "Look at you," I purr, tasting him. "I've barely started."

His hands twitch, but he still doesn't grab me. He lets me lead. Lets me take. And hell, the power of it sings through my blood like lightning.

I take him whole again, one slow inch at a time. He

groans, chokes on it, and finally, finally, I feel him start to rock into my mouth, surrendering piece by piece. His hips flex. His hands find my hair, but there's no force in them. Only reverence.

"You're dangerous," he pants, voice cracking. "Fucking deadly."

I hum around him, sending a fresh wave of tension through his body. His control is hanging on by a thread, and I'm the one holding the scissors. I love that feeling. So I pump my mouth up and down his huge cock, pushing him past my throat, even if I'm tearing up. The sensation to gag that I fight because I want to own him... that sensation is engulfing me. To ensure he never forgets this moment.

He stiffens, his fingers tightening around my hair, his cock suddenly super hard, and then he bursts. Filling my mouth with cum.

He growls. "Fuck me!" His whole body jerks as I gulp down every last drop of him, working it down my throat. I let him feel it, the way I own this moment.

I keep sucking even after the last drop for a bit of teasing, which leaves me growling. I pull back and lick my lips, chin slick, pulse racing. I glance up at him, and this time, he looks hollowed out. Worshipful. Absolutely stunning.

"I never wanted you to stop," I whisper, voice drowning with need.

He stares down at me, chest heaving like a man who just got devoured and fucking loved it.

I grind my slick thighs together, aching and unashamed. "I've never been so turned on before," I admit with a raw throat.

He doesn't respond right away. He just drops to his knees in front of me, eyes burning. "I think I've been yours since the first time you looked at me in the mansion like you could ruin me. And gods help me"—he cups my face, brushing his thumb over my swollen lips—"I want you to."

"I never want to stop bringing you pleasure." I have no idea if it's me or the hunger inside of me talking, but I'm so lost to him.

Ash stares at me like he already knows.

"You were a good girl," he murmurs. "Taking control like that. Making me beg with my body when I swore I never would."

His mouth finds the shell of my ear, and I gasp as his lips brush it, sending a shiver down to the backs of my knees. "But now..." he whispers, "it's my turn."

He draws back just enough to meet my gaze. "Will you be mine?"

The words crack something open in me. The ache flares hotter, sharper, more desperate. The wolf inside me purrs for him. And yet some piece of me, a fierce, unbroken, sarcastic piece, still claws its way out.

I smirk up at him.

"You're awfully polite for someone who keeps me naked in the woods."

His grin is feral, low and dangerous, like it wants to swallow me whole. "Say it."

I tilt my head. "Say what?"

"You know what," he growls.

Help me, but I do. "Yes, Master."

That grin turns lethal. "I fucking love that."

Before I can catch another breath, he moves—swift and sure. He lifts me into his arms, lays me down on the jacket he'd spread earlier, and stretches out over me like he belongs there. Like I'm his.

"You don't need control," he breathes, kissing the center of my chest. "You need to be adored."

He kneels between my thighs and pushes my legs up and open, high and wide, exposing everything. The cool air grazes my inner thighs, but it's nothing compared to the heat in his gaze.

His hand slides down between my legs, and he groans.

"You're gushing," he murmurs, almost to himself. "Drenched. Fucking perfect."

Two fingers slide inside me without warning, slick sounds echoing as he pumps them deep, watching my face twist with pleasure. My hips rise to meet him, desperate for more, and I cry out, panting.

"You're ready to be taken," he growls. "So I will."

The pressure disappears, and I moan at the loss.

But then he's there, his cock, heavy and rock solid once more, nudging against my entrance.

The stretch when he presses in is sharp and brutal and perfect. There's no teasing. No slow slide. He sinks into me in one deep, claiming thrust, and my breath punches out of my lungs.

I clutch the jacket beneath me, body arching, needing more even as I reel from the fullness.

"Let me fuck that innocence from you," he snarls.

"Master—don't be gentle," I gasp, grinding up to meet him, dizzy with need. "Please."

He drives into me harder, deeper, and every inch of him rubs me in all the ways I didn't know I craved. My thighs shake as he sets a punishing rhythm, and all I can do is take it.

"You were made for this," he pants, voice harsh and trembling. "Tightest fucking body I've ever had."

I groan, loud and wanton, completely lost. "I'm yours," I whisper. "I'm so yours. I'll never forgive you unless you fuck me so deep I forget my name."

He chuckles. One hand grips my throat, not to choke, just to hold, and he leans closer, sweat dripping down his temples as he slams into me again.

"I want to ruin you," he growls, dark and reverent. "I want to own every breath you take."

"You do," I choke out, body thrumming with pleasure. "Master, I want that too."

I don't know when the tears start falling. From

overstimulation. From the release building too fast. From the way this man is dragging me to pieces and putting me back together with every thrust.

He fucks me harder, and I can't stop the scream that tears from my throat. Slick is everywhere, dripping down my thighs, coating his cock. The sounds are obscene and relentless. My back arches, clenching, orgasm ripping through me so violently I swear I black out for a second.

He doesn't stop.

"I'm on the draea charm pill," I breathe, dazed.

His hips stutter. "I wasn't going to pull out unless you really wanted me to."

And then he groans, lowering his body flush against mine, pounding into me with a hunger that burns. His mouth finds my neck. "This is the start of everything we were meant to be."

My body quakes beneath him, raw and soaked, and I feel myself spiraling again, clenching around him as he fucks me through it.

His lips graze my ear as he whispers, "I was sent here to find my mate."

My breath catches.

"And I think I've just found her."

My eyes widen, but then his hips jerk, and he growls, deep and broken, as he comes inside me. Pulse after pulse, thick and hot, filling me until I'm gasping from the sensation.

He doesn't pull out. Doesn't move. Just holds me there, shaking, stretched, claimed.

"I want to carve my name into your soul, pretty girl," he murmurs. "So you'll never remember anything else but me."

My whole body shudders. His words should worry me, except here I am swooning, holding on to him.

And when he finally pulls out of me, we collapse across his jacket. He wraps me in his arms like I'm something sacred. His lips find my cheek, then my temple.

"Hey, gorgeous," he whispers. "How are you doing?"

"Never felt anything like this in my life." I glance at him, smirking, and he steals a quick kiss.

My pulse is still too fast. My thoughts, too loud. I try to make sense of it all, not just the sex, though that's its own entire spiral, but the shift, the wolf, and the man beside me who somehow took command of my body with a single look and made me want it.

His arm tightens around me as if he can feel me slipping away already. "I meant every word I said earlier."

My breath catches again.

No one has ever spoken to me like that before. Like I'm not just a moment or a body, but something that matters.

And of course, it has to come from the man I barely

know, the one I met after I'd just arrived at the party and a shift that nearly tore me apart.

I sit up, brushing pine needles from my thighs and pretending I'm not still buzzing from everything that just happened.

He watches me for a moment, something turning behind his eyes. "As I was saying earlier, before you bewitched me with your beauty and body, I think we switched abilities from a spell cast by that witch in the mansion. From the apple you threw at me."

My brows rise, realizing how I haven't had any ghostly visitors in a while.

I smile despite myself. "She said you were rude. That you needed a lesson."

He huffs, muttering under his breath. "Fucking witches. Come on. Let's go find her and get this fixed. And then..."

I narrow my eyes. "Then?"

"Then," he repeats with a sly smile, "maybe we can take more time to get to know each other."

"You want that?"

His gaze softens just enough to sting. "You don't seem to listen when I say something, so I'll say it again. I keep my word, and I want you. I think we're connected by more than some enchantment or some lesson."

My heart stutters.

I look away before I can do something reckless like

fall for him twice in one night. "There's just one issue," I say, trying to sound casual. "The spell the witch gave me said my mate's name starts with a *C*."

He blinks once, then chuckles, a deep, low sound. "What?"

He shifts to his feet and pulls something from the back pocket of his pants. A folded handkerchief. He crouches again in front of me, nudging my knees apart slightly. I tense.

"What are you—"

He's already wiping me clean. Gently. Quickly. Like it's the most natural thing in the world.

My mouth opens, but no sound comes out.

No guy has ever done that.

Not one.

He finishes and stuffs the cloth into a pocket of his pants. Then he helps me to my feet before pulling his jacket on me and buttoning it up. It swallows me, long enough to cover me past mid-thigh. The fabric is warm from us lying on it, and it smells intoxicating like him... delicious.

I stare at him, stunned.

"Okay," I mutter. "Who are you?"

He grins and leans in like he's about to kiss me, but instead he whispers against my ear, "My real name is Cassius. But everyone calls me Ash."

My mouth drops open.

He winks, looking entirely too pleased with himself.

"No way." I blink. "No. Freaking. Way."

"Told you," he says, standing and stretching. "You never listen."

"Cassius," I repeat, testing the sound.

He smirks.

"That's just unfair," I say. "You're hot, mysterious, cursed, and prophecy-approved?"

"What can I say? I'm the whole damn package."

I snort a laugh.

"And you're glowing," he says. "Which is impressive, considering you've got pine needles in your hair."

I smack his arm, and he just chuckles. He pulls his pants up, zipping them up, then grabs his shirt. He dusts it off before putting it on.

In no time, we're walking, laughter trailing behind us. The jacket shifts with every step I take, brushing my bare legs. The night feels beyond surreal, and I'm convinced I'm dreaming it all.

We move slowly, the distant pulse of party music threading through the trees. If I weren't barefoot and half dressed, I could almost pretend we were just another couple sneaking off for some fun.

But the wolf is quiet in my mind now, lulled and watching.

Still, I can't ignore the way the night hums around us.

A branch snaps ahead of us.

We stop.

From the shadows between the trees, two shapes step into view. Not drunk. Not playful.

They're armed. Dressed in dark leathers. Faces mostly hidden.

One of them points directly at Ash.

"You fucker," he growls. "There you are."

Ash doesn't flinch.

But I do.

Because I'm suddenly very aware that this night isn't done screwing with us.

CHAPTER
FOUR

ASH

The afterglow of what just happened with Erynn lasts approximately three minutes before everything goes to shit. Because of course my past comes knocking.

"The great Ash Valderson, alone in the woods with his whore," says the asshole, Cain, who steps out of the shadows ahead of me with his brother.

I should have picked up his scent before he reached us unannounced. I know that damn stench that accompanies the Bruck pack—rotted meat and old blood.

I push Erynn behind me in one smooth motion, scanning the night for any more of his men. But it's only the two of them, stepping forward with the casual arrogance of fuckers who think they've already won.

Cain is built like a brick shithouse, scarred face that even his mother couldn't love, and eyes that hold all the warmth of a frozen grave. His younger brother, Tobias, flanks him, smaller but faster. Both are dressed in black with heavy boots.

Erynn is huddled close against my back. I sense her there, not moving, exactly where I want her right now.

"Gentlemen," I bark, hands forming into fists at my sides. "Didn't realize the invitation said plus-two for assholes."

"Oh, this is perfect," Mikael says, materializing beside me with his usual terrible timing. "The Bruck brothers. Remember when Cain tried to court Jessica? She said she'd rather fuck a cactus. Good times." I huff a laugh, realizing no one else knows why. But fuck, I missed Mikael. Even dead and snarky, there's something grounding about having him at my side again.

"Heard you were here," Cain continues, stepping slowly to my left while Tobias mirrors him on the right. "Thought we'd settle some old debts. You cost us several warriors in that raid last spring."

"You mean where you attacked a training school for pups?" My hands flex. "Where you tried to take children as leverage? That raid? Where you also killed my second-in-command, Mikael?" I growl.

Tobias spits on the ground. "You slaughtered our people too."

"Should've slaughtered more," Mikael comments. "Starting with these two."

"Your people chose to attack children," I growl, ignoring my helpful ghost commentator. "They got what they deserved."

Cain's nostrils flare, and his head tilts. "The fuck is wrong with your scent? You smell…" He inhales deeper, confusion flickering across his scarred features. "Wrong. Broken."

Then his attention shifts to Erynn, behind me, and his entire demeanor changes. "But she smells interesting. Wolf, but not. Yours, but not quite." A cruel smile spreads across his face. "You got yourself a mate, Valderson? Perfect. She'll scream so pretty when we're done with her. Let you watch before we take your head. Then your pack is ours."

"Over my dead fucking body," I snarl.

"I can help," Erynn whispers behind me, and I feel her shift forward.

"No." I don't take my eyes off the brothers, but whisper over my shoulder, "You can barely control him. Stay back."

"Listen to your Alpha, little bitch," Tobias taunts, already starting to shift, bones cracking and reshaping. "Won't matter anyway. We'll have our fun with you both."

My skin crawls, rage igniting like wildfire in my blood. I should have ended these two when I had the chance. I wanted to. But now the universe is handing me the knife and daring me not to twist it.

"Oh, I have ideas for these two," Mikael mutters, floating between the brothers with vindictive glee. "You could shove Cain's head so far up his own ass he'd be wearing himself as a hat. Or—oh, this is good—remember that move with the spine and the—"

Cain lunges mid-shift, three hundred pounds of fur and fury aimed straight at my throat.

I shove Erynn to the side, my heels digging into the ground, weight dropping, shoulder forward—bracing for impact. There's no time to think, only react.

A snarl tears from Cain's throat a split second before his bulk collides with mine.

The force is brutal. I'm thrown back, air knocked from my lungs, body skidding across the dirt.

Cain is on me before I can suck in a breath, all teeth and claws and hatred.

But I'm already reaching, my fingers closing around the hilt of my blade still sheathed at my side.

Come on, come on.

Cain's jaws snap down, aiming for my throat.

I twist hard, just enough to make him miss, his fangs grazing air instead of flesh.

The dodge gives me one precious heartbeat.

Steel clears the sheath with a hiss.

I drive the blade up toward his ribs, aiming to gut him.

But Cain jerks sideways at the last second. The edge catches him across the flank instead, slicing shallow through skin and fur.

Blood spatters. He yelps, then growls, circling back.

My wolf is silent. But my fury isn't.

"Come on, then," I snarl, voice low and venomous. "Let's see if either of you bastards can fight without a spine."

Tobias comes from the right while I'm extended, jaws snapping for my dagger. I pivot, bringing my knee up into his throat, feeling cartilage crunch. He gags, stumbling back, but Cain has already recovered, returning with murder in his yellow eyes.

"Watch out," Erynn calls out.

"Behind you!" Mikael shouts, and I drop just as Tobias launches himself at me, but now he's aiming for Erynn.

"No!" I roar, spinning to intercept, but Cain's massive paw catches me across the chest, claws raking through fabric and flesh.

White-hot agony tears through me, and then I'm airborne, back slamming into a tree hard enough to steal my breath.

Stars burst behind my eyes. I drop to one knee, lungs screaming, chest on fire.

Fuck.

No fast healing. No wolf to knit the torn muscle or

dull the pain. Every inch of the damage is like fire. Flesh torn. Blood dripping.

I brace a hand against the dirt, force myself up.

They're still coming. And I don't have the luxury of staying down.

Erynn doesn't run. The stubborn, beautiful fool stands her ground as Tobias stalks toward her, transforming back into his human form, lips pulled back in a grotesque approximation of a smile.

"Come here, pretty thing," Tobias growls, and I fucking see that smug bastard's hard-on.

Fury punches me in the gut.

"Let me show you what real wolves do to—"

She moves fast. My wolf's power threads through her limbs, but not quickly enough.

Tobias backhands her. The crack of flesh on flesh is sickening.

She crumples, crying out.

That sound—

It rips straight through my chest.

No. I shove myself to stand steady despite the injuries, and lunge.

Except Cain barrels toward me from the side in the same moment. I don't have time to think, only move. I pivot, blade flashing, too late to dodge. His weight slams into me, claws digging in, but I twist with the impact, drive my blade up hard against his ribs.

Warm blood sprays my hand. He lets out a sharp,

strangled yelp and stumbles back, pawing at the wound.

I don't wait.

I whip around, Tobias looming over Erynn.

My insides snap, when suddenly, I stumble on my steps. *Wait, is that me?*

The ground trembles once more...

And this time, it's not rage.

"Uh, Ash?" Mikael's voice cuts through the chaos, stripped of all humor. "What was that? Even I felt it."

I don't answer. I'm already moving, pushing through the quaking earth, through the pounding in my skull. Nothing matters but her.

Tobias yanks Erynn up by the hair.

"After I'm done with you, maybe I'll keep you. Make you watch while we hunt down—"

I slam into him, shoulder to his side. He stumbles, snarling, releasing Erynn. I don't let him recover. I drive my knee into his back. Bone pops. He crumples with a howl.

I swing my fist down, cracking it against the back of his skull. He groans, collapsing flat. Not dead. Not yet. But he'll stay down.

I reach for her. She's on the ground, arms wrapped around herself, trembling. "Ash" is the only word that comes out.

"I've got you. Don't worry," I reassure her.

The world shifts beneath us once more. A low

groan rises again from the earth itself, louder this time, ancient and unnatural.

She stares up at me, eyes wide, pupils blown, whispering, "Ash… I think something bad is about to happen."

I don't have a response.

Then Cain is on me again, a blur of rage and blood, and I spin just in time to meet him, my blade raised. We clash and fall to the ground, him still in wolf form.

Suddenly, I catch movement from the corner of my eye.

Three figures claw their way from the earth like nightmares given form.

The first is mostly skeletal, patches of mummified flesh clinging to yellowed bones, wearing the rotted remains of what might have been a suit from decades past. Its jaw hangs loose, connected by strips of dried sinew, and when it moves, bones click and scrape like broken wind chimes.

The second has more flesh but maybe wishes it didn't as skin slides off in gray-green sheets, revealing muscle that's turned to jelly, eyes that have liquefied and run down its cheeks like tears of rot. It wears a dress that might have once been white, now stained with every fluid a body can produce as it decomposes.

Even Cain has paused, attention locked on the terror before us.

The third is the worst because it's the freshest

corpse, maybe dead only weeks, skin purplish black and split at the seams, revealing writhing masses of... things inside.

Cain whimpers, scrambling back on all fours in his human form now.

"It's you, Ash!" Erynn shouts. "Ash, you called them! Your anger, your need for help... You need to control the power."

"Zombies?" Mikael asks. "You raised fucking zombies. That's new. Also terrifying. I'm dead, and even I'm creeped out."

"I sure as fuck didn't mean to!" I climb to my feet as the corpses shuffle forward, their movements too fast for things that dead, joints bending in ways that shouldn't be possible.

"Tell them where to go!" Cain yells, backing away from Tobias, who's trying to get up despite bleeding from my attack.

"They need a mission, or they'll go on a rampage!" Erynn instructs, sounding as panicked as I feel. "They'll come after everyone, including us!"

"Ash, do it!" Mikael blurts out the obvious.

"How do I—"

The skeletal one lunges at Cain lightning fast. He yelps and dodges, but the corpse's bony fingers catch his hair, yanking him back. He goes ballistic, fighting it... screaming. "Get it off me! Get it fucking off me!"

"Command them!" Erynn shouts. "Like an Alpha

command but for the dead! Focus your will, give them purpose, or they'll just destroy everything!"

I try to focus, to find that place inside where Alpha commands come from, but it's different without my wolf. "Stop! I command you to stop!"

Nothing. If anything, they get more aggressive. The purple-skinned one has grabbed Tobias by the leg, and the sound he makes as its rotting fingers dig in will haunt me forever.

"Ew," Erynn states, moving to my side.

"Not 'stop'!" she corrects, her hand on my arm grounding me. "They came to help, so give them something to help with! And you have to mean it, feel it, push your will into them!"

"What the hell have you become?" Cain snarls, breaking free from the zombie, face pale, retreating quickly. But the skeletal corpse advances on him, jaw unhinging wider.

"Good question," Mikael chirps. "I'm going with necromancer. Or maybe death wizard? Ooh, corpse commander has a nice ring to it."

"Not helping, Mikael," I murmur. I close my eyes, dig deep, and find something that's not my wolf but sits in the same space. It's cold where the wolf was warm, patient where the wolf was aggressive. I push everything into my voice: "TAKE THEM. The two male wolves. Take them, and do not harm the woman or me. TAKE THEM NOW."

The change is instant. The corpses' heads snap toward the Bruck brothers in perfect synchronization, and then they travel forward, not shuffling but rushing, bones and rot moving with terrifying purpose.

Tobias scrambles and tries to run. The purple corpse catches him in three strides, bearing down on him. His screams cut off as putrid fingers find his throat.

Cain makes it farther, almost to the tree line, before the skeletal one and the flesh-sloughing one bring him down together. The sound of him being overwhelmed by the dead is wet and final.

"Oh, fuck!" Erynn breathes, clutching my side, both of us unable to look away from the carnage.

"That's disgusting," Mikael observes with fascination. "Is it eating his face? I think it's eating his face. Oh, wait, no, that's his—yep, definitely eating his face now."

"They'll return to their graves once the mission is complete," Erynn explains. "Usually. Probably."

"Have you ever raised the dead before?" I ask her.

"Technically, I raised a dead hamster once when I was seven," she states, and I turn to stare at her. "It was an accident. I was crying over Mr. Whiskers, and suddenly he wasn't dead anymore. Except he also bit through his cage and terrorized our village for three days before I figured out how to send him back."

"A zombie hamster."

"It ate the neighbor's dog." She shudders. "We had to relocate the following week. No one would come near our house after that."

The corpses are finishing their grisly work, and as we watch, they begin to sink back into the earth, taking what's left of the brothers with them. Within moments, the only signs of violence are the blood-soaked ground and the echo of screams in the air.

"So," Mikael says cheerfully. "You can raise the dead. That's fun. Totally not terrifying at all. Hey, think you could raise me? I mean, more than I already am? Maybe give me a body so I can drink again? I miss vodka."

I slump against the nearest tree, adrenaline crashing. "I raised fucking zombies."

"You saved us," Erynn corrects, wrapping her arms around me.

"This is so much worse than seeing ghosts," I admit.

"Or better, depending on your perspective," she says. "Do you know how useful combat zombies could be?"

"Please don't give me ideas."

Silence. We just stand there. Me. The woman I'm falling for, who has my wolf in her. My best friend, the ghost. And memories of the fucking undead coming back.

"This is the weirdest night of my life," I say.

"I have no words," Erynn adds.

"And it's not even midnight yet," Mikael contributes.

I wrap an arm around Erynn, who hasn't let go of me yet. For this moment, we're alive, we're together.

Could be worse.

Probably.

FIVE

ERYNN

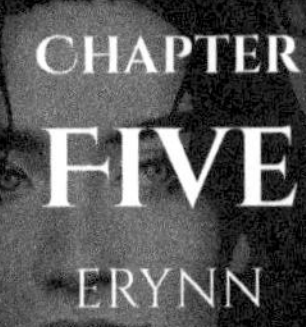

"We're completely fucked if we don't figure out this power shift, aren't we?" Ash asks, voice low, eyes scanning the trees like they're hiding the next horror.

"Still freaking out over the zombie thing?" I ask, trying to keep my voice casual, even though everything in me is stretched tight.

He gives me a look. Dry. Flat. Deadpan. Like I've just asked if water is wet.

"Okay, fair," I mutter, and then— "Ow. Fuck!"

Pain lances up my foot. I stagger, biting down a hiss, and glance lower to find a small thorn in the side of my foot. I reach for it and pluck it out. Ash is there before I can blink, crouching, his hands already on me, checking my foot and pulling out another small thorn.

"I got it," he says. Then he lifts me into his arms

like I weigh nothing. I should protest that this is ridiculous, over the top, but instead I end up curled against his chest, his jacket around me and the warmth of his body seeping into mine.

"Romance novels lied," I say against his throat. "They make barefoot forest wandering sound dreamy."

His chest vibrates with a low laugh. He shifts me slightly in his arms, like he wants me closer. His fingers flex along my thigh, steadying me, but it feels like more than that. Like he wants me here. Like I belong.

"You okay?" he murmurs, and when I tilt my head, he's already watching me.

Gods, that look.

It's not just hunger. It's not even just need. It's that deep, captivated stare that has my lungs feeling too full, as though he's trying to memorize every inch of me.

I remember the woods. His mouth on mine. His hands. The way he fucked me. My legs around his waist, the way I burned for him.

Did that really happen?

My body says yes. The ache between my thighs says yes. The wolf in me growls his agreement, rolling in contentment like he knows we were claimed in more than just instinct.

His gaze drops to my lips.

"You're staring," I whisper.

"You're warm," he says back as if that explains it. "And you smell like you're mine."

His jaw ticks, like he wants to kiss me again.

I don't pull away.

Because in his arms, I don't feel lost or confused. I feel safe.

And maybe that's more dangerous than anything I've ever faced. I glance away before I burn up, taking in the forest.

"Oh!" I spot something glinting in the moonlight, desperate to shift the focus from the ache behind Ash's eyes. "My shoe!"

It's one of my heels, somehow miraculously still intact. The strap is caked in mud, and there's something dark dried across the sole, but it's there. The other lies a few feet away, looking like a corpse on a battlefield. Fitting, honestly.

Ash stops walking and lowers me to my feet before he crouches and picks them up, turning them over in his hands.

"These are completely impractical."

"They weren't meant for running from the undead," I say. "They are made to make my legs look good."

His eyes flick up, sharp and unwavering. "Your legs are spectacular without them."

"You're flirting with me while holding my shoes?"

"Is it working?"

I only grin as he scoops me back into his arms and keeps on walking. We're near the edge of the woods now, the cracked stone path ahead with moonlight reflected in pale streaks. He sets me down again and kneels in front of me, still holding the shoes.

"Foot."

"I can put them on myself."

"Foot." That voice. That tone. It's not a request. It's a command.

I mutter something under my breath but lift my foot anyway, steadying myself with one hand on his shoulder. He's warm through the fabric. Solid. My mind flashes back to his body over mine in the trees, breath against my throat, his weight pinning me perfectly.

"Focus," he murmurs without looking up.

I bite my lip.

He fits the heel gently to my foot, fingers adjusting the strap with far too much precision for a man who can break ribs with a single punch. His thumb brushes against the arch of my ankle. I shiver.

He repeats the process with the other shoe, his hands lingering again. When he finishes, he doesn't rise. Just stays there. Kneeling in front of me, breathing shallow, jaw tight. The moon highlights the cuts and dried blood on his face.

"We look like hell," I say, trying to break the quiet.

"Me in your oversized jacket, you looking like you got dragged through several levels of monster-infested hell."

"It's Halloween," he says, but the words sound like someone else is speaking through him. "Old tradition said humans wore masks to scare away spirits. We'll just say these are our costumes. You're a half-naked forest witch. I'm a warrior who lost a fight with a sentient bramble."

His head cants slightly, like he's tracking something only he can sense. His lips move, soundless... There's a flicker of pain in his expression so sharp it slices through the moment. I feel it like a needle under my skin.

"Who are you talking to? A ghost?" I ask, all too familiar with spirits turning up at the most inopportune times.

He doesn't look at me, but something shifts, and he stands up from his crouching position. A tension unwinds in his shoulders, his jaw slackening for just a breath before his entire body slumps—like someone cut his strings.

"It's Mikael in ghost form, my best friend, my second-in-command," he reveals roughly. "Don't tell him, but I miss him so fucking much."

The words splinter on their way out. He presses his fists against his sides, his back bowed as tremors ripple through him. Silent grief, the kind that eats people alive from the inside out.

"I lost a handful of my pack that night," he mutters. "Mikael was the closest thing I had to a brother. And I let him die."

"Ash—"

"He called my name while the enemy pack tore him apart," he says, his voice going dead flat. "And I didn't go. I stayed where I was. Held the line. Watched him fall."

Silence stretches between us, the forest holding its breath, as though even the trees know not to interrupt.

"You had to make a choice," I whisper, reaching for him. "You stayed for the others—"

"Don't," he snaps. But it's not cruel. It's cracked glass. "Don't forgive me. Not yet."

His head finally turns. His eyes lock on mine. They're piercing, amber, haunted, as if he's trying to brand this moment into both of us. And maybe he is. Maybe he's trying to make me find the monster he believes he is.

But all I see is a man unraveling, holding too much pain in too little space.

I move closer, sliding behind him and wrapping my arms around his body. "I've only known you for a night," I murmur against his shoulder, "but I've seen enough to know you don't need punishment. You need someone to stay."

He breathes deeply. Then he exhales, and his whole body shudders.

"Mikael thinks I'm an idiot for blaming myself," he states finally. "Says saving the kids was worth it. Says he would've made the same call. Then he makes it weird and says that you have a nice ass."

I blink. "Wait, what?"

"He's still here," Ash says dryly. "Still annoying. Still has no boundaries."

"I—well—tell him thank you, but if he tries to float at me suggestively, I'm calling a priest."

"He says that you blush easily, and I have to agree."

I shove at his shoulder. "Your dead best friend is hitting on me?"

"Vigorously." He chuckles and turns to face me, both of us standing so close that his breath washes over my cheek.

"Never tried kicking a ghost in the balls. But I'm willing to find out what happens if I do."

That earns me a low laugh. It slips through his teeth like he forgot how to make the sound.

"Otherwise, how are you dealing with... my power?" I ask, softer now. "And not having your wolf?"

His gaze meets mine like he's weighing how much to give me.

"It's like I'm an empty vessel," he admits. "Like he's just behind a wall I can't break through."

I watch his throat bob as he swallows hard.

"Your wolf misses you," I whisper.

Ash goes still. His gaze darkens.

His voice is low. "You feel his emotions too?"

I nod.

He glances away for a moment. "The first time I changed, I was thirteen. Got lost in the ravine during a storm, soaked through, scared shitless. Thought I was going to die. But then... it happened. The shift. Bones snapped, skin tore—and it should've been agony, but it was right."

He pauses.

"I remember the first breath I took in wolf form. How sharp everything was. The scents. The sounds. The freedom. I wasn't afraid anymore. I wasn't alone."

My chest tightens.

"That was the night I knew," he continues. "I'd kill for my pack. Protect them. Lead them, if I had to. Not because I wanted power. But because they mattered."

His words scream loyalty, pride, and violence just under the surface, held in check by the love he has for the wolves that follow him.

"I admire that," I admit. "You lead like it's a sacred duty."

He studies me again, this time with something raw flickering behind his gaze. "You don't scare easily, do you?"

"Not when it comes to you."

A slow smirk touches his lips. It fades quickly.

"What's it like?" he asks. "Your magic. Because right now it feels like I've got a live wire running through my whole body. Every nerve is humming. And I feel so much colder than usual."

I snort. "And the sensation of having something alive inside me feels freaky."

He chuckles as if he agrees. A dark sound, low in his throat, and it does something to me. My toes curl inside my heels.

His hand finds mine again, fingers threading through like he owns it. As if he owns me. His grip is firm. Possessive. And when we step onto the stone path, he pulls me closer to his side.

"I'm not letting you get away from me," he murmurs, voice hot against my ear.

My pulse skitters. I don't pull away.

Because part of me doesn't want to be anywhere but at his side.

And the wolf inside me? He's already home.

Ash doesn't let go of my hand as we move through the side garden, taking us on a path to the front of the mansion. Leaves crunch under our feet. The pulse of the party vibrates through the ground, the thrum of music, laughter, distant howls of wolves. I glance down at myself and wince. The jacket I'm wearing falls just below mid-thigh and hangs loose on my frame, gaping enough to flash cleavage. But Ash walks like he owns the damn place.

He's on a mission, as am I, to find a way to switch our powers back.

We enter the mansion through a side door, and I'm immediately reminded of how opulent this place is. A few people stare at us... me in nothing but a man's jacket and heels, him in a shirt that is scratched and streaked in blood. Yet, he holds his head high, hand firmly holding mine, absolutely zero fucks given about our appearance.

A true Alpha, even without his wolf.

"Erynn! Oh my gods!" Sera's voice cuts through the ballroom's noise like a siren, and suddenly she's in front of us, eyes bulging as she takes in our appearance. Her dress is slightly askew, her elaborate hairdo has fallen to one side, and there's a hickey on her neck.

"Walk of shame, party edition," she states, her gaze sweeping over us. She's practically vibrating with excitement, bouncing on her toes. "Like, where is your dress? That beautiful blue number I spent an hour helping you into? Or did he go all animalistic on you? Did he rip it off? Because that's fucking hot. Girl, he is HOT."

"Sera, breathe," I manage, face burning hotter than Phoenix Fire.

"Hello," Ash says with amusement in his tone. "And everything here is for Erynn only."

"Possessive already? I love it." Sera claps her hands. "Rich! Rich, come see! Erynn got laid!"

My face might be bright red. "Please stop talking," I beg.

Rich appears beside her like smoke, taking us in. He's got a new bruise on his jaw that wasn't there earlier, and his knuckles are split. We aren't the only ones who got into a fight.

"Rich," Sera declares, wrapping herself around him like a vine. "This is Erynn's... friend."

"Ash," Ash supplies, offering his hand. The men shake, and I watch them do that thing where they try to establish dominance through grip strength.

"You look like you've had an interesting evening," Rich observes, taking in our disheveled state with barely concealed amusement.

"Halloween brings out the interesting in people," Ash replies smoothly, pulling me closer to his side. I love how he does that, casual but deliberate, like he needs me within arm's reach at all times.

"Let me get us all drinks," Rich offers, pressing a kiss to Sera's temple that's surprisingly tender. "You two look like you could use something strong."

"Give us a moment," I say quickly. "We need to find someone first, then we'll come back for that drink."

Sera blinks at me. "You're voluntarily leaving a social situation with me... to go find someone? That's new."

"The night's been… educational," I say, which is the understatement of the century.

"I'll bet," she smirks. "That's a lot of education written all over your neck."

I touch my throat automatically, feeling the tender spots where Ash was particularly enthusiastic earlier.

"We should go," Ash states, his hand warm on my lower back. "Before we miss her."

"Her?" Sera's eyebrows rise. "Is this a threesome situation? Because I need details. All the details. Preferably with diagrams."

"It's not—no," I stammer. "Definitely not that."

"Pity," Rich says with a perfectly straight face. "Threesomes can be very educational."

Sera smacks his arm. "When have you ever had a threesome?"

"Wouldn't you like to know?"

"I would, actually. When? With who? Why wasn't I invited?"

As they bicker, Ash leans down to my ear. "Spotted her. Far wall, near the windows. Let's go see the witch."

I follow his gaze across the ballroom to where a small crowd has gathered near the tall windows that overlook the gardens. She's there, mostly keeping to herself. She seems to glow slightly, or maybe it's just the way the light hits her silver hair.

"Rain check on those drinks," Ash tells Rich, already guiding me away.

"Don't do anything I wouldn't do!" Sera calls after us.

"That's not very limiting," I call back.

"Exactly why it's perfect advice!"

Ash keeps his hand on my back as we navigate through the crowd. People are definitely staring at us now. I try to channel some of that confidence, keeping my head high even though I'm very aware that this jacket barely covers everything it needs to.

"You good?" Ash asks quietly.

"Yep. Ready to do this," I say, only half sarcastic. But my pulse skips anyway.

Because this is it. The whole reason we came back.

I want to believe this is just a conversation. That she'll nod and agree and wave her hand and unravel the curse like it's nothing. But deep down, I know that's not how these things work.

She is sitting on a chair, legs crossed, a sleek black cocktail glass dangling from her fingers as she watches the crowd like she's selecting her next meal.

My skin prickles. Every fine hair on my arms lifts like static has rolled through me. My wolf goes still. Not in fear. In warning.

Ash doesn't react. Of course he doesn't. He can't feel it. Not anymore.

But I can.

I do.

That heavy, low thrum in the air. Like gravity is bending just slightly wrong.

Not party tricks. Not sleight of hand.

This is power that presses behind your eyes and whispers to your blood.

The witch looks up before we even reach her.

Her gaze snaps to mine, violet and gleaming with interest. Her lips curve slowly, like she's been waiting for something and we're finally it.

"Well," she says, voice smooth and amused. "You certainly took your time."

Ash steps forward. "We need to talk to you."

She grins. "I imagine you do."

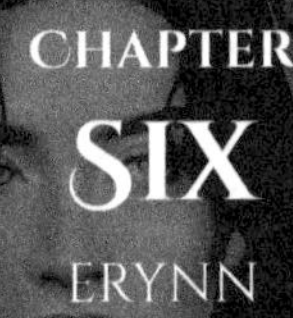

CHAPTER

SIX

ERYNN

Ash stiffens beside me. The wolf in my head responds to him, hackles rising, but I squeeze his hand in warning. The last thing we need is to piss off the witch and end up with something worse than a power swap.

"Learned your lessons yet?" she asks, focusing on Ash with intensity. She meant every word of teaching him a lesson from earlier.

"Yes," I quickly say, before he can say something that'll get us turned into toads, or worse. "That's why we're here. Please, how do we fix this? How do we go back to how we were?"

She takes a languid sip of her drink, the blue liquid leaving a faint glow on her lips. "Fix? Such an ugly word. Implies something's broken."

"You cursed us," Ash says flatly.

She lifts one perfectly sculpted brow, clearly amused rather than offended. "*Cursed* is such a harsh word too. I'd say... Expanded. Gifted with perspective."

"Gifted?" Ash's voice drops to a growl that would be more impressive if he actually had his wolf.

I nudge Ash lightly with my elbow and step forward. His fingers twitch like he wants to stop me, but he doesn't. The wolf bristles under my skin. He doesn't trust the witch, and neither do I, but he knows when to beg.

"Please," I say, trying for a smile that isn't all teeth. "We've had a really shitty night. Lesson learned, big-time. Whatever you did with the apple, can you just... undo it? Reverse it?"

The witch watches me over the rim of her cocktail, her expression unreadable. She sets the glass down on a small table beside her with a soft clink and folds her hands in her lap, one elegant wrist draped over the other like a lady waiting for a suitor to grovel harder.

"Oh, sweetheart," she says. "It was never meant to last. It'll unravel on its own, when it's ready. Halloween always holds on to its gifts stronger."

Ash exhales harshly through his nose, and his shoulders coil tighter. "Then end it now," he snaps, voice as sharp as broken bone. "We can't afford to wait. This isn't just some magical inconvenience. I have responsibilities—"

"He runs a pack," I cut in. "And if they see him like

this, if they sense weakness, they'll tear him apart. This is dangerous," I explain to the witch. "Not to mention, my day job relies on my ability."

The wolf pushes against my insides again.

The woman doesn't flinch. If anything, her smile softens. It's the worst part. Like she expected this. Like she's heard it all before.

"I do understand," she says at last. "But before I give you what you want, I need something in return. A little insight, perhaps."

I glance at Ash, who's already shaking his head, but I squeeze his hand once. His fingers twitch, then settle.

The witch pats the chairs beside her.

"Sit. Humor me."

We pull the chairs around to face her and settle down.

The witch crosses one leg over the other and leans forward, eyes gleaming.

"First question," she begins, her voice a touch lower. "In the heat of anger, when you were sure the other was to blame, did you choose rage, or did you find room for grace?"

Ash doesn't speak right away. He stares at the ground. His fingers flex in his lap.

Finally, he lifts his head. "I was furious. At her. At myself. At everything. We were both spelled, both caught in something bigger than us, but I acted like I was the only one affected." He scrubs a hand over his face. "I didn't explain. Didn't try to help her understand what was happening to her. I just expected her to cope with it like I would have. Which was... stupid."

"And yet?" the witch prompts, eyes glinting like starlight through smoke.

"She didn't give up," he says quietly. "She stayed. Fought. Even when she lost control and begged me to fuc—"

"Oh my god," I interrupt, burying my face in my hands. "That does not need to be part of this conversation."

Ash only shrugs, maddeningly unbothered. "It was beautiful and hot."

"I will strangle you," I say through my fingers jokingly.

The witch chuckles. "I do enjoy a couple that can argue like lovers and enemies in the same breath."

"I wouldn't call us a couple," I start, but Ash leans closer, his knee brushing mine deliberately.

"You're really bad at lying, sweetheart," he whispers.

I swat at his leg. "You're impossible."

"And you," the witch says, staring at me.

I shift slightly, uncomfortable. "Well, he made me furious. So many times. He was cold, sharp-tongued, impossible to read. But then... he stopped running from what was happening to us. He stopped trying to fight it, and started trying to fix it. To understand me." I glance at Ash and then back at her. "When my wolf spiraled, when I was losing control, he didn't just restrain me. He anchored me. He trusted me to get through it. And when the ghosts came for him, I noticed how much he dealt with it head-on. It's not just brooding. And tonight... I guess I saw past the anger. Past the curse. I saw him."

Our eyes meet across the sliver of space between us. His expression is unreadable, but something in me knots up anyway. I don't know what he's thinking, but I know what I feel. My pulse stutters. My mouth is dry. And I hate how much I want to scoot closer, to feel the heat of him again, just to see if it still settles the storm in my chest. Like some part of me is already rewriting the rules, deciding he's not just a mistake I survived... but someone I'd choose, even now.

"My second question," she says, distracting me. "Let's imagine something improbable, yet not impossible. Say she finds out she is carrying your child. What do you do?"

My breath catches, and I blink at her, stunned. "What kind of question—"

Ash's hand settles firmly on my thigh. "She moves in with me. Immediately. She gets the entire damn castle and whatever else she wants. I raise that child with her, side by side. I become the father they need.

And if she wants it"—his thumb brushes over the fabric of my jacket—"the husband she deserves."

My mouth falls open. "Really? You'd do all that?"

His gaze slides to mine, calm and unwavering. "For you? I'd do anything."

We stare at each other, the world narrowing down to the weight of that answer, the absolute certainty in his tone. No hesitation. No fear.

A long moment passes before I say softly, "Okay. Wow. That's... good to know."

The witch only watches us, her smile widening. "Delightful," she murmurs, sipping from her drink like this is the best kind of theater.

Then her gaze sharpens. "Final question."

The air shifts again to something darker. "You've tasted each other's gifts. What did you each embrace? And what, if anything, could you not live with?"

Ash is quiet for a moment. Then he exhales.

"I embraced the dead," he groans. "Not because I wanted to. But because I had no choice and got to see my dead friend Mikael again." His throat bobs. "He's my ghost. My mistake. But... seeing him gave me something I didn't know I needed. Facing the past instead of hiding from it."

I turn to him, reaching for his hand, holding it.

The witch nods once, acknowledging the weight of his response.

"And what can you not live with?" she asks.

Ash is glancing at me, and this time, there's something raw behind his eyes. "What I can't live with," he says quietly, "is taking my wolf back and losing Erynn in the process. She's not just carrying part of me; she is part of me now. My wolf responds to her like she belongs. Like she always did. I didn't expect that. And I sure as hell didn't plan for it... but I can't imagine going back to the way things were before."

I close my eyes, absorbing that, my toes curling in my shoes at the words he's saying, words I don't expect.

Then I answer. "I embraced the wild," I admit. "His wolf. The strength. The instincts. It's in me now, and it's... maddening sometimes, but it's real. I can feel how deeply the wolf cares and what it's like living with something inside of you."

Ash's jaw tightens slightly at that, but he says nothing.

"And I can't live with the silence," I continue. "With not hearing the dead anymore. That's who I am. It's how I connect with the world. With people that others forget. It's like losing a part of myself." I glance at Ash. "And I get it now. I didn't before, but I do now. That... emptiness. When something so core to you is just gone."

His gaze locks with mine, and the air shifts. His fingers trace along my jaw, a slow glide that has me catching my breath. When he reaches my lips, his touch lingers, featherlight, and I swear I sense my pulse beneath his fingertips. My heart trips over itself as heat blooms in my chest, my skin, everywhere. He leans in, and I tilt toward him instinctively, dizzy with the pull of him. Is he going to kiss me?

A half sigh, half-amused hum draws both our gazes sharply to the side.

The witch leans back, her eyes alight like she's just tasted something rich and rare. "You've both answered honestly to each other."

"So we passed your test. We danced to your tune. What now?"

Her smile turns wicked. "Since you asked so nicely..."

She rises before us. "There is a way to release what binds you sooner. But it requires intention. And... cooperation."

"You'll need to perform a ritual together. One that acknowledges your bond, honors your pain, and surrenders the pieces of each other still inside you."

The wolf inside me stirs uneasily. "What kind of ritual?"

"Not the sort that ends in fire and chanting," she says dryly. "Think of it as a... communion. A confession. You've already begun. You just need to finish it with truth."

Ash lifts his chin. "Tell us what to do."

"Oh," the witch hums, retrieving a scroll from the

folds of her impossible dress. "I think you'll figure it out."

She presses it into my hands, then steps back with a grin too wide to be friendly.

"Witching hour closes in," she adds. "Don't wait too long." She starts to leave, then pauses for a moment, casting one last look over her shoulder. "Not all monsters show in the mirror, but the reflection always tells the truth, if you're brave enough to look."

And just like that, she vanishes into the crowds.

Ash and I are left with the scroll between us, silence settling like fog.

I glance at him. "You still ready to do this?"

His hand finds mine again.

"Now more than ever."

Ash breaks the seal immediately, unrolling the parchment. We both lean in to read it.

The page is completely blank.

"Is this a fucking joke?" Ash growls, and this time the sound is purely human frustration.

I take the parchment from him, holding it up to the light. Nothing. Turn it over, still nothing. Hold it at an angle, squint at it, even sniff it, and absolutely zilch.

"There's nothing here," I admit, trying to keep the accusation out of my voice and mostly failing.

"Reflection," Ash mutters. "She mentioned some cryptic message about reflection?"

"Mirrors," I say. "They could show our message on the parchment."

We search the ballroom first, and the mirrors here are all decorative and gilt-framed, so we both move quickly to the one closest to us at the rear of the ballroom.

I lift the page to the mirror, and we both stare into its reflection.

"Fuck!" Ash is frowning.

The parchment stays stubbornly blank.

"She did say 'witching hour.' That's three a.m.," I explain, slumping against a wall. "Maybe we just have to wait."

Ash checks his watch. "It's only one thirty. We have time to kill."

"Well, I can't kill it dressed like this." I gesture at myself—his jacket, which barely covers the essentials, and shoes that have definitely seen better days. "I need clothes. Real clothes."

"I don't know." He almost purrs the words. "I'm rather fond of this look."

"Of course you are. It's your jacket."

"It looks better on you."

"Everything would look better on me right now. A potato sack would be an improvement."

Ash glances at me for a long pause. "Stay here," he orders. "I might have a solution. Something that'll cover you up better."

And then he disappears into the ballroom crowd, leaving me to lean against a wall and try not to feel too exposed. The wolf is restless, pacing inside me, wanting to find him. It's disturbing how quickly I've gotten attached to Ash's presence, how wrong it feels when he's not near.

He returns carrying a dress, deep green silk that actually looks like it might fit. "Found this in the coat check. Someone left it with a note saying 'For whoever needs it more.'"

"That's either very kind or very cursed."

"Only one way to find out."

I slip into a nearby powder room to change, and miracle of miracles, the dress fits perfectly. It's simple but elegant—long sleeves, hem that hits just above my knees with a sexy slit up the side of my leg, low back that shows the scratches I definitely don't remember getting. When I emerge, Ash's expression makes the whole cursed night worth it.

"You look..." he starts, then stops, seemingly at a loss for words.

"Like a person wearing actual clothes?"

"Beautiful. Stunning. Hypnotic," he says simply, and the sincerity in his voice has me blushing.

"You need a new shirt," I deflect, but my voice comes out breathier than intended.

He takes the jacket from my hands and slides it on, tucking the parchment paper into its pocket. "This will do. Now, let's pretend we're just two people at a party. No curse, no power swap, no zombies in the woods."

"That's a lot of pretending."

"I'm very good at faking it." He offers me his arm. "Dance with me?"

"I should warn you—I'm terrible at it. Two left feet, no sense of rhythm, and a tendency to step on toes."

"Perfect. I have a tendency to lead whether my partner wants me to or not."

We step onto the dance floor, where the party is somehow more intense. The music is darker now, thrumming with bass that I feel in my bones. Bodies press together, and more than a few couples are definitely doing more than dancing in the shadows.

Ash pulls me into the crowd, and I discover that he wasn't lying about the leading thing. He moves with the kind of confidence that makes up for my complete lack of coordination, his hand resting low on my back, just shy of indecent, as he guides me through the steps. Every touch sends heat pooling low in my belly.

When I stumble, he catches me easily, palm sliding along my waist, fingers brushing the side of my breast like it's nothing. Like he doesn't notice. But the way his eyes darken says otherwise. My pulse skitters. I let out a breathless laugh, and his grin flashes in return, wolfish, knowing.

He leans in, lips grazing the shell of my ear. "I want

you to know that I meant everything I said back there. With the witch."

My smile fades into something softer, needier. I can't meet his eyes without feeling scorched. "Me too," I finally admit. "And I'm letting you take the lead," I murmur, not referring to just the dancing anymore.

His fingers flex at my waist, tugging me a fraction closer, until the press of our bodies turns the dance into something else entirely. My chest brushes his with every breath. Heat bursts low in my stomach, and I stop pretending this is just about movement.

"Where did you learn to dance?" I gasp, breath fluttering across his ear as the music swells around us.

"Pack gatherings," he murmurs, his voice rough and warm against my neck. "My mother insisted all young wolves learn. Said it was about knowing how to move with a partner. Reading their body. Trusting the rhythm. Giving in, taking control, sometimes both at once."

"Sounds like she knew her stuff."

"She did." His hand skims lower, dragging me closer. "She's gone. But she's in everything I do." He grins, eyes glinting.

Before I can answer, he twirls me out, spinning me with ease, then draws me back in so fast I stumble, landing flush against his chest. His face is inches from mine. His breath is mine. His gaze drops to my lips.

And then he kisses me.

It's not a gentle brush. It's deep and slow and claiming. My knees weaken, hands gripping his shoulders, needing him to hold me up and never let go.

A loud whistle cracks through the haze.

"Get it, girl! That's my girl, Erynn!" Sera suddenly yells from across the dance floor. "You two look like you're about to scandalize the entire ballroom."

I pull back, laughing into Ash's shoulder. He grins and wraps his arms around me, tucking me into him like he has no intention of letting go anytime soon.

"Tell me something about yourself," he asks, mouth against my hair. "Something real. Just yours."

I hesitate, then tilt my head to look up at him. "I used to live in a little red house tucked deep in the Finnish forest. Quiet. Secluded. You could hear the wolves howling at night."

His brow lifts slightly. "Which forest?"

"North of Lake Saimaa."

He goes still, fingers tightening slightly at my waist. "You're kidding."

"What?"

"I grew up in those same woods." He leans in, brushing his nose along my cheek. "My pack's land is on the other side of the ridge."

I blink up at him, stunned. "You're from Finland?"

"Born and raised. Middle of nowhere. Closest neighbor was probably your ghosts."

My breath hitches, and I can't help the smile that

slips free. "So all this time... I was listening to your pack from across the ridge?"

He grins, full and bright, eyes flashing gold for just a second. "Fate, huh? Maybe not as cruel as we thought."

He twirls me gently beneath his arm, catching me close, and this time his hand settles low on my back again. Our bodies press together, and I feel the heat of him through every point of contact.

"Tell me something else," he murmurs, lips brushing the curve of my jaw like a secret. "Something that has nothing to do with ghosts or tonight."

I try to think through the pounding of my heart. "I moved to Helsinki for a job with the Nordic Institute of Posthumous Communications."

His hand tightens just slightly, his thumb sweeping a slow stroke over my spine. "You left the forest for the city?"

"Yeah," I murmur. "The silence got too loud with too many ghosts." I pause, then glance up at him. "You know those woods are controlled by the Dukes, right?"

His brow lifts. "The mercenary brothers."

I nod. "Khaos, Eryx, and Tallis. Half brothers. Dangerous, rich, and ruthless. Everyone in the north has heard of them. They run the biggest mercenary operation around... and their grandfather, part god, still pulls strings behind the scenes."

Ash lets out a low hum, something like amusement. "Yeah, I know them. Did some work for them years back—tracking, intel, protection gigs. They've settled now, believe it or not. Found their mate, Billie. Had twins."

I blink. "Seriously?"

"Seriously. Wildest part? They're good fathers."

Ash pulls me closer again, and now there's no space left between us. His thigh presses between mine as we move, our rhythm slower, deeper. I feel his breath on my cheek, his mouth so close to mine.

"Your family still out there?" he asks.

"Not really. My parents never quite accepted me for what I am. The ghosts scared them. I scared them. It was only my grandmother who had the same ability as me."

He hums, his lips brushing the edge of my cheekbone. "Their loss. If they'd known what they were letting go of..."

I tilt my face toward him, drawn in by heat and gravity. His gaze drops to my lips. For a second, I think he's going to kiss me again—

"Remind me to thank the witch for cursing us," he murmurs instead.

I glance up at him through my lashes, heart racing. "Maybe she wasn't so bad after all."

He dips his head again, brushing his lips against the shell of my ear. "You are so beautiful."

A tremor slips down my spine. It's not the curse.

It's not even the residual energy of the dead pressing at the edges of the ballroom. It's him.

I go still, breath stuttering in my chest, like my heart is caught between beats. "You shouldn't say things like that."

"Why not?" he murmurs. "Because I meant them?"

I pull back just far enough to look up at him. His face is too close. His eyes are molten.

"Because I might believe you," I whisper.

The corner of his mouth lifts, but it's not his usual smirk. It's quieter. Hungrier. "Then maybe I should say them again."

His hand shifts on my waist, drawing me in as the music slows again. We move, swaying lazily. My body remembers this too well, his fire, his nakedness, his scent, the way he made me orgasm and scream.

Every brush of our bodies, every turn, feels slower. More deliberate. We're not dancing anymore. We're orbiting. Colliding.

I shouldn't want this. Not like this. He's a stranger. I met him tonight, under a curse, and yet he feels carved from some forgotten part of me.

I try to force logic into my voice. "This is crazy."

"I know." His gaze drops to my mouth. "And yet."

I laugh, soft and nervous, and glance away. "Come on," I say, tugging his hand. "I need a drink before you do something worse than raise the dead."

He huffs a quiet laugh and lets me lead him off

the dance floor, his palm hot against mine. We weave between masked dancers and towering candelabras until we find a tall cocktail table near the edge of the room, half shadowed by velvet drapes.

"Sit," he says, pulling out one of the high-backed chairs for me.

I climb onto the seat, suddenly very aware of the length of my bare legs from the high split in my green dress.

He leans down slightly, his voice close. "What's your poison?"

"Surprise me."

He flags down a server. A minute later, a pale pink cocktail appears in front of me, garnished with sugared berries. He takes a whiskey for himself and leans against the table beside me, the glass balanced between his fingers.

"To surviving the night," he says.

I clink my glass to his. "We're not done yet."

We drink. His eyes never leave me.

After a beat, he sets his whiskey down. "So tell me, is talking to ghosts really a full-time job?"

"You'd be surprised," I say, taking a longer sip than necessary. "Inheritance disputes, missing persons cases, cold-case murders. The dead know things, and the living pay a lot to hear them."

He raises a brow. "Ever solve any murders?"

"Three. Well, two and a half. The half was acciden-tal. I was trying to find someone's missing cat."

His lips twitch. "Let me guess. Ghost cat?"

"No, living cat. Mr. Mittens. The ghost was the murder victim. Turns out Mr. Mittens witnessed the whole thing and led me straight to the body."

"Mr. Mittens and Mr. Whiskers," he says, eyes gleaming. "You've got a theme."

"I didn't name them!"

He leans in, voice dropping. "Sure you didn't."

A laugh slips out before I can stop it. I shake my head and knock back more of the drink. It's strong. Fruity with a sharp bite. Like him.

His expression shifts. "How do you make them stop? The ghosts. They're always talking. Whispering."

"You learn to tune them out," I say. "Like back-ground noise."

I set my drink down and reach for his hand. He doesn't flinch. Doesn't hesitate. Just watches me with steady curiosity as I spread his fingers wide.

"Feel that?" I ask. "That buzz in the air? Cold and electric and hungry?"

He nods.

"Now imagine a wall. Not solid. More like mesh. A filter. It lets you know they're there without letting them in."

His eyes darken with focus. Slowly, the air around us stills. The pressure fades, just enough.

"That's better," he says. "They're still there, but quieter."

"It takes practice." I let go of his hand, but his fingers linger against mine. "The wolf is the same, right? Always there, but you control when it surfaces?"

"Usually," he says. His gaze drops, slowly dragging over me, from the fall of my hair to the bare skin of my thigh in the slit that goes all the way up to just below my bikini line. "It's impossible to think around you, you know that?"

My breath catches.

He leans in more and takes a deep inhale.

I don't move. I don't breathe. The silence between us grows taut and trembling.

"That's you drawn to your wolf talking."

His eyes meet mine. "Is it?"

God help me, I don't know.

A nearby clock chimes. We both turn.

"It's almost three," he says, and I had no idea time had passed so quickly.

I nod but don't look away from him. "Time to check the mirrors."

He straightens, but not before brushing his fingers against my knee. Not quite an accident. Not quite innocent.

He holds out his hand. I take it.

And we step into the crowd.

We make our way back to the alcove with the most

mirrors. The music has shifted to something almost mournful, and there are still lots of people at the party.

"Two fifty-eight," Ash states, checking his watch.

I pull out the blank parchment from his jacket's pocket and lift it to the mirror. Still nothing. Though something worrying flares in my stomach. What if this doesn't work?

"Maybe at exactly three o'clock?"

We wait, watching the second hand tick closer. Two fifty-nine. *Three. Two. One.*

"Now," I breathe, holding the parchment steady.

Nothing.

"Fuck!" Ash growls, and I don't blame him.

"Maybe we're doing it wrong," I say. "Maybe 'reflection' means something else. Self-reflection? Reflecting on the night?"

"Or maybe she lied." Ash stares at the mirror like it has personally betrayed him. "Maybe this is permanent."

The wolf in my head gives a mournful whine at the defeat in his tone, and something in me tightens in response. Not just the wolf. Me. Erynn. The woman who walked into this place with ghosts whispering at her heels and a job built entirely on hearing them. Who would she be without that? Not a medium. Not a guide for the dead. Just... ordinary.

The thought lands hard. Heavier than I expected. I've always known who I was. What I was. My ability wasn't just part of me; it defined me. Gave me purpose. Identity. Without it, who would come to me? Who would need me?

A hollow ache grows in my chest, sharp and sudden. If the curse is permanent, I lose more than my connection to the dead. I lose myself.

"I don't want to be stuck like this," I whisper, staring at my hands. "I've only ever been the girl who hears ghosts. It's all I know. If I lose that... I don't know what's left of me."

Ash reaches out, his fingers curling gently around mine. Not just comforting, but grounding.

"You're more than that," he says. "I know we only just met, but tonight... it doesn't feel like I'm talking to a stranger."

I glance up, startled by the sincerity in his voice. He's watching me with a furrowed brow, a faint crease between his eyebrows.

"Is it weird that I feel like I know you better than half the people in my life?" I murmur. "Like... all those conversations and awkward dinners with coworkers, and none of it felt like this. Like any of it mattered." Well, except, Sera... She's like my sister.

"I don't think it's weird," he answers softly. "You see people differently when you're cursed together."

I laugh out loud. "So what now?"

He doesn't answer right away. Just lifts our joined hands and turns them so his thumb brushes the inside of my wrist. Light touch. Barely there. But it sends heat curling through my belly.

"We'll figure it out," he says. "Together." He studies me for a beat too long. His gaze isn't intense. It's... open. Like he's letting me see all the thoughts behind it.

"Together," I repeat. "And after?"

The words that pour out catch me off guard. I blink, trapped between now and then.

"When we're back to normal?" he adds, still tracing slow circles on my skin.

I want to answer. Want to tell him something hopeful or funny or clever. But all I can do is picture my empty apartment. The silence. The lack of footsteps that aren't mine. The ghosts that used to be there and might not be anymore.

I swallow hard. "Let's solve one crisis at a time."

He leans in. Just enough that his breath skims the side of my throat. "That wasn't a no."

My chest flutters again, nerves and warmth colliding. I lean forward without realizing it. The wolf in my head stills, calm and content in a way I've never felt before.

Then he lifts his wrist, showing me his watch.

Three thirty.

Nothing changes.

We both freeze. Expecting something. A shift. A sign.

But the silence stretches long and hollow.

Nothing.

Still cursed.

Still stuck.

Still... too close for comfort.

"This is insane," I say with a broken laugh, but it comes out all sharp, laced with fear. "What if this is it? What if the witch *was* just screwing with us? What if there's no way back?"

He squeezes my hand. "Don't say that."

I'm pacing now, my shoes clicking against the old tile. "No, seriously. What if it's all just some cosmic joke? My life is built on talking to the dead, Ash. That's how I help people. It's who I am."

He's quiet for a moment, then stands. Walks over. Gathers me into his arms like it's the most natural thing in the world. "Then we find a new path. Together."

I close my eyes and let myself fall into his warmth.

"Maybe we missed something," I whisper against his chest. "Reflection. What if it's something else completely?"

"Perhaps we've been looking for answers in the wrong places."

Without another word, we rush to the doors. The air outside is colder than before, damp with dew, carrying the faint metallic bite of predawn. We are hurrying into the woods, deeper, when somewhere in the distance, water trickles.

We follow it.

A narrow stone path winds through a hedge maze we hadn't noticed before.

Around a bend, we reach a shallow stone basin— almost like a fountain, except it's still. Perfectly still.

And in it, the moon stares back.

Not broken by ripples. Not disturbed.

Reflection.

I exhale sharply. "There. That has to be it."

Ash takes a step forward, then another.

"I really hope this works," I say, heart thundering.

"Because if it doesn't?"

"Then I guess we live here now. Cursed and confused."

He reaches for my hand again. "At least we wouldn't be alone."

I stare down into the water, watching my reflection blur and shift beside his.

And something is wrong.

The wolf in my head growls low.

Ash stiffens.

This has to be the reflection the witch was talking about...

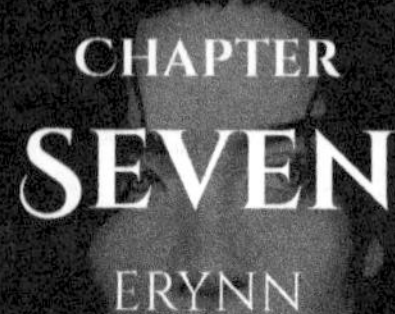

We're both staring into the water, and I immediately wish we weren't.

The pool is wrong in every possible way. Too still, too dark, too perfect in its reflection of the moon overhead. It's like looking into liquid obsidian, if obsidian could judge you and find you wanting. The surface doesn't ripple, doesn't move, doesn't even seem to breathe. It's the kind of still that makes you want to throw something in just to prove it's actually water and not a portal to somewhere where teeth live.

"This is giving me serious horror vibes," I mutter, gripping Ash's hand tighter. His palm is warm against mine, the only warm thing in this clearing. "Where everyone knows looking in the cursed mirror is a terrible idea but they do it anyway because the plot demands their stupidity?"

"And then they die horribly," Ash finishes, his thumb brushing over my knuckles in what might be comfort or might be him checking that I'm still solid and real. "While screaming about how they should have listened to the warnings."

"Exactly. And there are always warnings. Usually from a creepy local who speaks in riddles and has cataracts."

"We had a creepy witch who spoke in riddles."

"No cataracts, though."

"That we could see."

"Fair point. Or maybe she had perfect vision and that was the real curse." I'm babbling, but looking at this pool has every instinct in me screaming that we should run. Now. Fast. And never stop. "So we agree that this is stupid?"

"Incredibly stupid," he confirms, but he's leaning forward anyway, drawn by what I assume is a terrible curiosity I'm suffering from too.

"But we're doing it anyway?"

"Obviously. We've come this far on bad decisions. Why stop now?"

My reflection stares back. It's normal at first, just me appearing exhausted and disheveled in a borrowed dress that's already showing signs of our trek through the woods. There's a leaf in my hair I didn't know about, and my makeup has given up entirely, leaving me with what Sera calls "raccoon chic."

Then my reflection smiles.

I definitely didn't smile.

Her eyes start to glow with this silver light like moonlight on morgue metal, and her smile keeps widening, showing too many teeth. Far too many teeth that belong in sharks' mouths, not human faces.

"Oh, fuck no," I breathe, but I can't look away. It's like she's got hooks in my eyes, keeping them locked on hers.

Ash makes a strangled sound beside me, and I risk a glance at his reflection.

Gods. Oh gods.

It's him but wrong, caught between forms, human face stretched over wolf bone structure, the geometry all off like someone tried to fold a person into an animal shape without removing any of the original parts. His jaw extends too far, packed with teeth that shouldn't fit, some human-flat, others wolf-sharp, creating this horrible, crowded mouth that looks as though it's in constant pain. His hands can't decide what they want to be, fingers elongating into claws and then shrinking back, bones breaking and re-forming in endless loops.

"That's not—" he starts, but his reflection grins, and the expression is pure darkness, pure wrong, pure nightmare fuel.

My reflection tilts her head, still grinning that awful smile, and mouths words I can't hear but somehow understand: *You're nothing without them.*

The *them* feels plural, feels like it means the ghosts, means Ash, means everyone who's ever mattered.

"Okay, backing away now," I say, but my body won't move. It's as though the pool has gravity, pulling us closer. "Ash? We should really stop looking at the creepy murder water."

"Agreed," he mutters, but he's not moving either. His jaw is clenched so tight I hear the grinding of his teeth.

Our reflections move in perfect synchronization, pressing their palms against the underside of the water's surface. The pool ripples—finally, movement —but it's wrong, moving upward like something is pushing from below.

"Look at you," my reflection says, and her voice drips contempt like honey laced with cyanide. "Playing dress-up in someone else's clothes, in someone else's life. You think he actually wants you? You're just convenient. Available. Here."

"Shut up," I whisper, but she keeps smirking.

"Without your gift, what are you? A mediocre employee with a dead houseplant collection and a ghost cat that isn't even yours. Your parents used to call twice a year out of obligation—your birthday and Christmas, and even then they kept it under five minutes. Your best friend had to convince you to come tonight because you'd rather sit at home reading about other people's lives than live your own."

The words strike me in the chest like precisely aimed arrows, each one finding its mark in my softest spots.

"Face it," she continues, her glow intensifying. "You're background noise in everyone else's story. The quirky friend. The weird girl who talks to dead people. Never the lead. Never the one who gets chosen."

My gut hurts, and I'm going to be sick.

Beside me, Ash is as rigid as stone, and I hear his reflection speaking too, that grinding voice full of cruelty.

"Dead pack members because you were too weak to save them all. You carry their names like prayer beads—Eero, Astrid, Jens, Björn, Ingrid, Olaf, Mikael—but prayer won't bring them back."

Ash flinches at each name, his hand tightening on mine until it almost hurts.

"Your father was right," his reflection continues. "You're soft. Playing at being Alpha while real wolves die for your mistakes. The pack whispers about it when you're not around. How many more have to die before they realize you're not strong enough?"

"Enough!" Ash bellows, but his reflection laughs, making this horrible sound like bones breaking.

"Even now, you can't protect her. You're standing

right there, and you can't stop what's coming. Just like with Mikael. Just like always. You'll watch her die too, and add another name to your litany of failures."

"I said, enough!" Ash roars, and the sound is barely human.

We stumble back from the pool simultaneously, breaking whatever hold it had on us. I'm breathing as if I've run through the woods, my chest heaving, heart hammering so hard I'm surprised it's not visible through the dress. Ash is panting too, perspiration on his brow, and when he glances at me, there's a wildness in his eyes that speaks of real fear.

"What the absolute fuck was that?" I gasp, bending over with my hands on my knees, trying not to vomit from the adrenaline surge. "Since when do reflections have opinions? Strong opinions? Rude ones? I didn't sign up for therapy via aggressive water spirits."

"Magic," Ash says grimly, but his voice is shaky. "The kind that knows exactly where to twist the knife."

"Yeah, well, magic can go fuck itself with a rusty spoon. Sideways. Twice." I straighten up, still trembling, wrapping my arms around myself. "Something feels really wrong here. More wrong than the general wrongness we've been dealing with all night. This is advanced wrong."

"It's trying to break us," he admits quietly. "Using our own fears against us."

"Well, it's doing a bang-up job. Five stars. Would recommend to enemies," I say.

That's when the parchment in Ash's hand flares with heat, making him curse, which sounds like it involves gods and fish and possibly someone's mother.

Words appear on the previously blank surface, writing themselves in what looks like liquid starlight:

To break the curse, speak your truth. Shed the lies that bind your soul. Only those who see themselves clearly can be free.

"Oh, good," I say, voice dripping enough sarcasm to fill the pond of water. "Vague mystical instructions. My favorite. Why can't magic ever just say 'Push this button, curse broken, have a nice life'?"

"Because that wouldn't be sufficiently traumatic," Ash replies, staring at the words like they might rearrange themselves into something helpful if he glares hard enough.

The wolf in me is pacing, agitated, wanting resolution.

"We have to go back to the water," Ash suggests, and I hate that he's right.

"I know." I take a breath that doesn't quite fill my lungs, like the air here is too thin or too thick or too something. "But if my reflection starts talking about my houseplant graveyard again, I'm fighting her. I don't care if she's made of water. I'll find a way."

"I'll help. We can take them together."

"Deal!"

"I want to help you fight anything that hurts you," he says simply, like it's obvious, like it doesn't make my chest feel too small for my heart.

"That's… that's actually really sweet. Stupid, but sweet. Stupidly sweet. Sweetly stupid."

"You're deflecting."

"Absolutely. It's that or cry, and my face is already a disaster without adding tears to the mix."

"You're beautiful," he confesses, and the sincerity in his voice almost undoes me.

"Now *you're* deflecting."

"I'm really not."

"We should—" I gesture vaguely at the pool, unable to finish the sentence because what we should do and what I want to do are very different things.

"Right. The curse. The breaking thereof."

We approach the pool again, slower this time, like we're approaching a wild animal. Or a bomb. Or a wild animal holding a bomb while juggling chainsaws.

Our reflections are waiting.

They look normal for exactly three seconds before the wrongness starts again. This time, I'm ready for it. Or as ready as anyone can be for their reflection to develop sentience and attitude problems.

"Back for more truth?" mine says, and her voice is clearer now, more present. "Here's one—you're terrified he'll leave. Everyone does. Your parents, emotionally. Your friends, gradually. Now him, inevitably."

The words sting because they're true. Every relationship I've ever had has had an expiration date, some faster than others. My parents still love me, I know they do, but they've always loved me from a safe distance. Like I'm radioactive. Like caring too much might infect them with whatever wrongness I carry.

"You're right," I say, and my voice only shakes a little. "I am terrified of being left again. Of not being enough to make someone stay. Of being the person everyone eventually realizes they can live without."

My reflection's smile falters slightly, like she wasn't expecting agreement.

"But here's what you're missing," I continue, finding strength in acknowledging the fear rather than fighting it. "I survived everyone who left. I built a life, maybe not a perfect one, but mine. I learned to be alone without being lonely. Well, mostly. Sundays are still rough. And holidays. And birthdays. Okay, so I haven't totally mastered it, but I'm working on it."

"Pretty words—" my reflection starts.

"I'm not done," I interrupt, which feels weird, interrupting myself, but here we are. "If I can be complete on my own, if I can function and survive and even sometimes thrive alone, then I can choose to be with someone without needing them to complete me. That's not desperation. That's choice. That's freedom."

"You think you're free?" She laughs, and it sounds like ice cracking. "You're bound by your gift, your fear, your desperate need to matter to someone, anyone—"

"True words," I cut her off again. "I talk to the dead for a living. I've learned that the only lies that really hurt are the ones we tell ourselves. And I've been telling myself I'm not enough for so long that I started believing it. But here's the thing—I'm scared, yeah. Terrified. But I'm here anyway. Standing by a cursed pool at three-something in the morning, facing my worst fears made manifest, because breaking this curse matters. He matters. We matter."

I squeeze Ash's hand, drawing strength from his solid presence. He does the same back, and I know he's watching, listening to me.

"That's not weakness," I continue, voice stronger now. "That's courage. That's choosing to try even when failure is not just possible but probable. That's human. And I'm human. Flawed and strange and sometimes I talk to my houseplants even though they're dead, but human."

My reflection ripples, distorts, the silver light in her eyes flickering like a dying bulb. For a moment, she's monstrous, all teeth and hunger and void, and then suddenly she's just me. Tired and scared but standing her ground, mascara smeared but chin up.

Ash turns to his own reflection.

"You want my truth?" His voice is steady, the Alpha one that makes people listen whether they want to or not. "The reality is I wake up every morning with their names in my throat. Seven names, seven faces, seven futures that ended because of my choice."

His reflection watches with those wrong eyes, patient as a spider.

"But here's the rest of that truth—forty-three children woke up this morning because of that same choice. Forty-three futures that exist because I was willing to carry seven ghosts." His voice strengthens, gaining power with each word. "My father would have let them all die rather than lose warriors. 'Acceptable losses,' he would have called them. Children. Babies. Acceptable losses."

"Pretty philosophy for a killer," his reflection says, teeth too sharp around the words.

"I *am* a killer," Ash agrees without flinching. "I've ended lives with my hands, my teeth, my choices. I've washed blood from my skin so many times I sometimes forget what clean feels like. But I've also saved lives. Protected them. Shielded the weak from the strong, the innocent from the guilty. The killing serves the protecting, not the other way around. That's what makes me different from my father."

"Different but not better—"

"Better," Ash says firmly. "Not perfect. Not even

good some days. But better. I choose to be better every day, even when it costs everything, even when it earns nothing but grief. That's not a weakness. That's a strength my father never understood."

His reflection shifts, normalizes, becomes just him, scarred and steady and absolutely certain.

The pool goes still again, perfectly mirror-still, and for a moment I think we've done it. Broken through whatever test this is, passed whatever cosmic final exam we've been taking all night.

Then the surface starts to bubble.

Not like boiling water, but like something massive is rising from depths that shouldn't exist in a shallow pool. As though this isn't really a pool at all but a window, and something on the other side has decided to come through.

"That's not good," I admit, backing up, pulling Ash with me. "That's very much not good."

The water explodes outward, but instead of getting us wet, it forms shapes in the air, shadows with weight. They swirl around us like a tornado of whispers, and I can hear words, phrases, accusations, each one in a different voice, some I recognize, others I don't:

Failure— —freak— —unwanted— —weak— —abandoned— —killer— —monster— —alone— —always alone— —why did you let me die— —should have been you—

The shadows press in, cold and invasive, trying to worm their way under my skin. It's like being embraced by every doubt I've ever had, every fear made manifest, every 3:00 a.m. thought given form and malice.

"Don't listen!" Ash shouts, pulling me against him, but the shadows are between us too, yanking at us to pry us apart with fingers made of ice.

He'll leave— —she'll run— —not enough— —never enough— —everyone leaves— —everyone dies—

"No!" I press my face against Ash's chest, his heartbeat hammering against my cheek. "I *am* enough. We *are* enough. I survived being alone, and I choose not to be. That's strength, not weakness. That's choice, not desperation."

"I protect because I can't not protect," Ash adds into my hair, his arms tight around me like he can shield me from incorporeal threats through sheer will.

The shadows actually shriek and pull at us harder. Something fundamental is starting to shift within me, like tectonic plates moving in my soul. The wolf in my head howls in distress, but it's not just being upset. There's something else. Anticipation? Fear? Recognition?

The death-cold in my bones flares to ice, but it's not leaving. It's... changing. Merging with something else, something warm and wild and alive.

And then—

Raw, unfiltered, impossible power flooding through me like someone opened a dam in my chest. This is hot and cold together, life and death wound into a double helix.

"Ash!" I gasp, and he's breathless too, doubling over but not letting go of me, never letting go.

"I feel strange," he hisses through gritted teeth. The shadows converge, slamming into us like a powerful force, being hit by a wall of frozen night. I hear myself screaming.

The darkness presses in from all sides.

Something is wrong.

The wolf howls in my ears, while Ash is bellowing something I can't make out from all the sounds in my head.

Then silence.

Nothing at all.

Just the dark, and the sense of falling, and the certainty that when we wake—if we wake—nothing will ever be the same again.

EIGHT

"Erynn! Erynn, wake up! Please wake up!"

Sera's voice cuts through the darkness like a dagger dipped in panic. Her hands are on my shoulders, shaking me hard enough to dislodge memories I didn't know I had. My head feels like it's been used to drum out a war chant.

"Five more minutes," I mumble, which comes out more like "f'mornins."

"You've been unconscious in the woods for gods know how long! This is not a five-more-minutes situation!"

Woods.

Right. The pool. The curse.

Ash.

My eyes snap open, and I immediately regret it. The low sunrise is offensively pretty, all golden fire and pink whispers kissing the trees like it has no idea what just happened here. My skull pounds in protest.

Sera's face swims into focus above me, lipstick long gone and her carefully sculpted updo now resembling the aftermath of a stylish lightning strike.

"Oh, thank the ancestors," she breathes, yanking me into a hug that makes every rib scream. "I've been looking everywhere for you. Rich disappeared, again, because apparently he's allergic to emotional responsibility, and you weren't in the mansion, and then I maybe sort of panicked and came out here searching for you."

"I-I must have passed out," I croak. My throat is so raw.

She pulls back to examine me, scanning my face.

"Are you okay? You look like death. More than usual, I mean."

I push myself upright, everything aching. The clearing looks... wrong. The pool is gone. Not drained. Not dried up. Just... gone. Like it was never here. Like the earth closed its mouth over a secret it wasn't supposed to share.

My heart stutters.

"Where's Ash?"

The words fall out sharp and too fast, betraying me.

Sera's face tightens.

"I only found you. I'm sorry, babe. I looked. I

swear. But there was no one else here. Everyone's left the party."

"Oh." The sound is too small, too hollow. I clear my throat. Try again, try for something casual, something cool.

"Oh, well. That's... that's fine. One-night stand with a mysterious Alpha in a haunted forest. Classic me. Very on-brand."

"Erynn—"

"No, seriously, it's fine."

I wave a hand like I'm brushing off a bug and not the first real connection I've had in years.

I stand, the green dress torn, dirt-streaked.

"These things happen, right? Guy says sweet nothings in the dark, makes you believe in moonlight and magic, and then poof. Gone. Typical fairy tale. With me cast as the girl who gets left behind."

"If it's any consolation, he didn't seem like the type to just vanish," Sera says.

"I'm sure they never do." I say it with a sharp little smile.

That's the trick, isn't it? They all seem different. Until they're not.

I brush a few leaves from my dress, tug the hem straight like I can press the dignity back into it. My hand trembles, just once, but I hide it. I always hide it.

"He's probably halfway back to his pack by now, curled up in some den with his wolves, regaling them with tales of the cursed party and the dumb girl who thought she was something special."

Sera steps in closer and pulls a leaf out of my hair. "You weren't dumb. And you are something special."

I don't answer. I can't.

Because if I open my mouth, I'm scared all the softness I've spent years bolting down will come pouring out.

A flicker of motion pulls my gaze to the trees. A spirit. A little girl in a tattered Gothic dress drifts between the trunks, her expression lost and confused. Child ghosts often look that way. I wait for the familiar chill to rise along my arms, the icy whisper of the dead that has always wrapped itself around me like a second skin.

My ability is back, and I smile to myself with the comfort of what I've always been accustomed to.

I close my eyes and search inward, reaching for the wolf who'd curled himself inside my head like he belonged there. But he's not there. Only a hollow space where he should be. I can't stop running my thoughts over it. Around the edges of that emptiness, something lingers. A presence. A thread tugging gently toward a place I can't see. A bond.

No. I'm not doing this.

I am not going to be the girl who builds entire futures around one night. Even if it was a night full of impossible things. Even if it changed everything. Even if it meant something.

My chest tightens. And if Ash is gone... if he chose to leave after everything we just went through...

Then maybe the truth is that I really am better off with ghosts.

At least they don't leave.

"Rich left too," Sera says quietly beside me, trying for solidarity. "Come when they want. Leave when they're done."

"They're the same," I admit. "Ash was just a guy. At a party. Who happened to save me from killer wolves, raise the dead, merge his soul with mine, and help me break an ancient curse. You know. Casual."

Sera doesn't laugh, but her lips twitch.

"Let's go home," I say, stepping back from the clearing.

She starts tracing symbols in the air, her fingers glowing with blood magic. Crimson sigils spark in the rising sunlight. Portal magic is delicate work. You need blood. Intent. And the kind of insurance that covers accidental transport into a stranger's bathtub.

"You sure you don't want to wait?" she asks softly. "Maybe he's just—"

"He's gone, Sera." I stare at the patch of dirt where the pool used to be. Where he and I were. "It was what it was. A weird, cursed night that's already over. We're back to normal now. Everything's fine."

"You keep saying 'fine' like if you say it enough times, it'll turn into truth."

"It's a legitimate coping mechanism."

"It's denial with extra steps."

The portal begins to form. A tear in the air opens, revealing my apartment's living room. My couch. My coffee table. My poor, dead plants that I forgot to water for two weeks straight. Everything just as I left it. Dull. Ordinary. Mine.

"How do you do it?" I ask, suddenly tired. "With Rich. How do you handle him leaving all the time?"

Sera pauses, one hand still glowing in midair. "I don't make attachments. Not the kind that hurt. I care about him, yeah. But I don't let myself need him. You can't lose something you never let yourself hold."

I nod slowly. "I didn't think I made attachments either. It was just one night."

She looks at me, sympathy softening her eyes. "Give yourself time."

"It was a mistake, apparently." My voice catches in my throat. "He left."

"Maybe he didn't."

"Can we just go? Please?"

She finishes the last symbol. The portal hums, its edge shimmering with quiet power. "After you."

I look back at the clearing one last time. At the space where everything happened. Where nothing will ever happen again. Some ridiculous part of me still expects to see him crashing through the trees, panting, explaining. Telling me it meant something.

But the forest only offers ghosts and silence.

I turn away. And step through.

The Nordic Institute of Posthumous Communications is exactly as I left it, aggressively modern, intimidatingly expensive, and full of people who deal with death like it's a particularly annoying customer service issue.

It's afternoon now. I managed maybe two hours of broken sleep, haunted by dreams of wolves and water and amber eyes. My third cup of coffee sits cooling on my desk while I stare at my calendar.

Mrs. Lindqvist. 2:00 p.m.

I sigh.

"Erynn," the receptionist's voice crackles through the intercom on my desk. "Your two o'clock is here."

"Thanks," I say, pushing back my chair.

The open-plan office hums with the usual blend of keyboard clicks, hushed conversations, and the occasional rustle of snack wrappers. I pass clusters of cubicles and glass-walled rooms. One of the meeting rooms has no glass walls, and that's the one I use.

Mrs. Lindqvist is waiting inside, seated on the low velvet couch like a queen on her throne.

She doesn't rise when I enter.

Today's outfit is different from the last time, less grieving widow, more victorious divorcée. Blood-red designer suit, diamonds around her neck and fingers, and a thin smile.

"Shall we begin?" she asks, crossing one leg over the other.

"Whenever you're ready." I close the door behind me and settle into the armchair across from her.

The air is warm, too warm, but the moment I reach for my gift, the temperature plummets. The veil parts easily, and the cold rushes in like a wave.

He appears instantly.

Mr. Lindqvist.

More solid than last time. More faded, too. Like someone crumpled him down and tried to smooth him back out.

Death has a way of stripping people bare. Turns out Erik Lindqvist was a very small man wearing a very expensive life.

"Tell her about Cyprus," he snaps without preamble.

"She already knows about Cyprus," I reply coolly.

Mrs. Lindqvist just smiles. "Oh, let's keep this short." She straightens on the couch. "I found everything, Erik. Cyprus, Cayman, Switzerland, even that little account in Malta you thought was so clever." She examines her manicure with satisfaction. "It's all mine now. Every penny you tried to hide and give to your other girlfriends."

Erik's ghost pales, which I wouldn't have thought was possible, considering how translucent he already is.

"That's not—she can't—"

"I also found out about Natasha," Mrs. Lindqvist says, casually brushing an invisible speck from her skirt.

"Who's Natasha?" I ask, though I already have a sinking feeling I don't want the answer.

"His other wife. In Monaco. Married her two years ago, apparently. Which makes our marriage technically invalid, but the lawyers say I still get everything, since he's dead and she's not legally recognized here."

Erik has the audacity to look sheepish. His ghost flickers, the edges of him sparking with indignation.

"It didn't mean I loved you any less," he says, his voice softer now, and I relay the words to his wife.

Yet, somehow, the words land on me like a stone. Can someone say they care and still vanish over and over? Still lie? Still carve out entire lives without you in them?

Ash's face flashes behind my eyes.

The way he looked at me.

The way he said he wouldn't let me out of his sight.

But he did. He's gone.

Just like everyone leaves.

Mrs. Lindqvist stands, movements graceful and decisive. The power radiating off her isn't magical, but it's powerful all the same.

"I don't actually care what his excuses are," she says, smoothing her jacket like she's brushing off the past. "This is the last time I'll be here. I just wanted him to know that despite all his lies, all his betrayals, all his pathetic attempts at hiding assets, I'm going to have an amazing life."

She glances around the room. Her gaze is steady, sharp as a blade.

"I'm going to spend your money, Erik, on things that would make you furious. I'm going to fuck men half your age on the yacht you loved more than me. I'm going to live, gloriously and vindictively, while you"—her voice drops into something cold and final—"are just dead."

Even I can't help it.

I grin.

Erik's ghost is vibrating, jaw clenched, hands fisting like he could do something about it.

He can't.

She's won.

And honestly? Good for her.

He vanishes like the wind, just like that.

Mrs. Lindqvist drops a small transparent bag of gold coins in my lap with enough wealth to pay for my rental for a year. "A tip just for you to buy yourself something nice, dear."

"Thank you so much."

Then she's gone, closing the door behind her, and I'm staring at the generous tip, deciding that Sera and I are going to take a holiday.

I stroll out of the meeting room, needing air. Or water. Or possibly something stronger. At my desk, I drop the coins into my bag, then go in search of Sera.

She's leaning against the reception desk with a grin that sets off every internal alarm.

"What're you up to?" I ask, eyeing her with suspicion.

"Me? Nothing. Innocent as a lamb. Pure as snow. Trustworthy as—"

"Sera."

She sighs, still smirking. "The boss wants to see you. Aurora Room."

My stomach drops.

The Aurora Room is our most exclusive consultation space, reserved for special clients or cases involving multiple spirits. Not where you get summoned for casual chats. Definitely not where you want to be called unexpectedly.

"What did I do?" I ask, heart thudding.

"Nothing. Just go." She winks. "Trust me."

I don't trust her when she's sly. I trust that grin even less. But I go, because my boss has been known to fire people for breathing too loud.

The door to the Aurora Room is shut. I knock. Wait. Then ease it open.

And freeze.

Ash is there.

Not my boss.

Ash.

He's standing by the window, city skyline behind him, sunlight catching the line of his jaw. He's showered, dressed, looking clean and whole and devastatingly handsome.

Like he didn't disappear into the woods. Like he didn't leave me.

My heart tries to climb into my throat. But I think of Mrs. Lindqvist, of diamond-hard women with knives for smiles, and I straighten my spine.

"Oh," I say, casually. "It's you."

He grins.

And damn it, my knees betray me.

"I thought I'd lost you," he admits. In three strides, he's in front of me. Close enough that I can smell his pine, smoke, and musk scent. Familiar. Dangerous.

"I told you last night," he murmurs, voice low, "I'm not letting you out of my sight."

"And yet," I reply, "you left me."

His smile falters. His jaw ticks.

"I woke up in wolf form. Deep in the woods. No memory of shifting. He'd taken over completely—wouldn't give me back control. Took hours to wrestle it away. He was... happy. Felt he was home." His hand lifts, presses against his chest. "Didn't think I needed to be in charge anymore."

Something inside me pulls tight.

That tether. The invisible thread I'd felt with his wolf.

"I'm sorry," he says, quieter now. "I didn't mean to leave you. You have to know that."

"So... your wolf kidnapped you?" I ask.

A small laugh huffs from him. "Pretty much." He glances down at his chest like he's having a word with himself. "I'm in charge. We find her first. Then you can run all you want."

I try to keep a straight face. I fail. I giggle. Actually giggle. "So you didn't abandon me?"

He shakes his head, stepping even closer. His hands lift to my face, palms warm, thumbs gentle. I lean into the touch without meaning to.

"I'd never do such a thing," he admits. "I couldn't. We're..." He hesitates, trying to find the right words. "Tied. Changed. You were part of me. I was part of you. Whatever we were before, it's not what we are now."

"Romantic," I whisper. "For a trained killer."

"I'm a man of many talents." His thumbs brush over my cheeks. "And, apparently, terrible timing."

"You think?"

"I remembered that you mentioned where you worked. Got back, told the pack I had a mate to collect—"

My eyebrows lift. "You told your pack?"

"Elders too. They're thrilled. Already planning the ceremony."

"Ceremony?"

"A Beta was picking out decorations. I didn't agree to that part."

My jaw drops. "Ash."

He shrugs, smiling like I'm the only thing worth looking at in the entire city. "I told them to calm down. First, I came to get you. But there's no rush."

"We barely know each other, though."

"Exactly," he says and steps back just enough to keep his hands cradling my face. "Which is why I'm taking you on a proper date tonight. After work. Dinner. Conversation. All the boring, beautiful things people do when they're not breaking curses and running for their lives."

I blink at him. "You want to go slow?"

"I want to do this right. We deserve that, don't you think? A chance to fall in love without magical inter-ference."

My heart makes an odd, fluttery lurch in my chest.

It feels like it's not just mine anymore. Like something in me recognizes something in him.

Then he's kissing me.

It's not like last night.

Not rushed. Not frantic. Not painted in fire and fear and hunger.

This kiss is warmth. It's steady hands and steady hearts. The way his lips move slowly against mine, like we have time. Like we're choosing this.

His hands tangle in my hair, pulling me closer, and I melt into him, completely and absolutely, until I feel that strange tether in my chest pulse, like it's content now. Like it's where I belong.

"I fell for you hard last night," he murmurs against my lips. "Half a day, and I missed you like a limb."

I smirk. "That's very codependent of you."

"We literally merged parts of our souls. I think codependency is implied."

He kisses me again, deeper this time, and I'm just sinking into the taste of him when giggling from outside the room breaks the moment.

I freeze.

So does he.

I turn slowly toward the door. Narrow my eyes. Then march across the room and fling it open.

Sera and three other colleagues all stumble backward, clearly guilty.

"Seriously?" I snap.

Sera straightens and tosses her hair. "We wanted to make sure you were okay."

"You wanted gossip."

"That too," she says brightly. "Also, I might have already ordered celebratory pastries."

I giggle, my cheeks already burning up.

Ash chuckles behind me, clearly enjoying this far too much.

"I hate all of you," I mutter.

"You love us," Sera says. "Almost as much as you love mysterious wolf boys with soulful eyes and a tragic backstory."

Ash leans in and whispers, "She's not wrong."

I nudge him in the ribs. He doesn't budge.

"You're all fired," I tell them.

"You don't have that power," Sera adds.

"I'll find it."

And despite the utter chaos of my life, my coworkers, the fact that I may have accidentally soul-bound myself to a werewolf in the woods, I can't stop smiling that he's returned for me.

Because maybe, just maybe, this is exactly where I'm supposed to be.

Ash steps behind me, arm sliding around my waist with casual possessiveness. "Nothing to hide. I'm hers if she'll have me."

"Let me think about it," I tease, but he's already tickling me, finding that spot just under my ribs that makes me squeal. "Okay, okay! Yes, I'll have you!"

"Good." He draws me against him, speaking into my ear loud enough for everyone to hear. "Because I have a lot to make up for. Leaving you in the woods, even accidentally, requires significant groveling."

"I do like songs."

"Then I'll commission a symphony."

Sera makes a gagging sound.

"We're not having this conversation in front of my office."

"Then let's have it at dinner." He presses a kiss to my temple. "I'll wait for you after work."

"Sounds perfect."

He kisses me again quickly, then heads for the front doors. Just before he disappears, he turns back with that smile that has my stomach somersaulting.

And then he's gone. Leaving me with a hallway full of grinning coworkers.

"So," Sera says, sidling up with zero shame. "He called you 'mate'!"

"Shut up."

"You're going to move to the woods for him."

"I'm not—maybe. Probably. Eventually. I don't know."

As everyone filters away, still buzzing about the office drama turned epic love story, Sera hugs me, whispering, "I'm so happy for you. You deserve the best." Then, with her grin, she heads to her desk, where a manager is waiting.

I drift back into the Aurora Room and edge closer to the window, staring out over the city.

The sun is setting, casting molten gold across the glass.

In a few hours, Ash will come pick me up for our first real date.

Tomorrow, we'll start unraveling what it means to be this... whatever we are. Soul-bound. Power-twisted. Dangerous. Unprecedented.

But for tonight, I'm just a girl who met a boy at a cursed party, traded magic and memories, and accidentally fell in love somewhere along the way.

The ghost of his wolf hums inside me.

My own power curls around it, cool and warm twined together.

For the first time in my life, I feel whole. Not because someone filled the missing pieces, but because I chose to share all of mine with someone just as broken and incomplete as I was.

It's a perfect beginning to an imperfect story.

But then again, the best stories always are.

EPILOGUE

ASH

The first snow of winter falls as I pace at the castle gates, and my wolf is practically vibrating with anticipation.

Six months of back and forth between the pack home and the city. Six months of my wolf whining every time we had to leave Erynn, of sleeping alone in a bed without her, of my pack giving me endless shit about being a lovesick puppy.

But today, finally, she's coming home.

"You're going to wear a groove in the stone," Rickon observes from where he's leaning against the gatepost, smirking.

"Shut up."

"The great Alpha, reduced to a nervous teenager. She's not due for another ten minutes."

"Traffic in the city could have been light."

Zac, head of my warriors, joins us with a steaming mug of something that smells medicinal. "He's been up since dawn, preparing her room."

"Our suite," I correct. "And I was checking that everything was perfect."

"You're pathetic," Rickon says fondly. "It's actually endearing."

I'm about to respond when I hear the hum of a magically powered vehicle navigating our private road in the woods. My wolf surges forward, and I have to physically stop him from spilling out and running to meet her. Ever since he shared her body, he's been ridiculously enthralled with her.

The car rounds the final bend, and there she is, visible through the window, staring at me with wide eyes. The vehicle stops, and she's out before I can reach for the door, launching herself into my arms with enough force to knock me back a step.

"Hi," she says against my chest, and that single word contains everything: I missed you, I'm here, we made it.

"Hi," I reply, breathing her in. "Welcome home."

She pulls back to stare at me, and her smile could power the entire castle. "I can't believe I'm finally here. No more long drives. No more portals eating my paycheck. Just... here."

"Just here," I agree, kissing her because I can't not. "Come on, let's head into our home."

Pack members are already unloading her bags, so many bags—where did they all come from?—while I take her hand and lead her through the gates.

She stops dead two steps inside.

"Every time I see the castle, it still leaves me breathless," she says. "I can't believe this is going to be where I live now."

I try to see it through her eyes. The central keep rises five stories, gray stone that's weathered eight hundred years of winters. We've modernized it, of course, with magical heating, running water, and electricity powered by a combination of solar panels and spelled generators, but we kept the bones intact. Towers at each corner, crenellations that once held archers now decorated with the pack's banners. The great hall's stained-glass windows catch the morning light, throwing rainbow patterns across the courtyard.

"We rebuilt it about fifty years ago," I explain as she gawks. "It was mostly in ruins when my grandfather found it. Took the entire pack working together to restore it."

"It's incredible." She spins in a slow circle, taking in the secondary buildings, the barracks for unmated wolves, the family cottages nestled among the trees, the stables visible in the distance. "How many people live here?"

"About two hundred full-time. More during gatherings." I slide an arm around her waist as a few more locals notice us. Pack members start drifting closer. "Everyone's excited to have you move in finally."

She snorts. "Oh god, how many ghost questions am I going to get?"

"So many. Sven's already got a list. His grandmother died last year, and he's convinced she hid money somewhere."

"He's probably right. Grandmothers always hide money. It's like a universal law. Tucked in an envelope, behind an ugly ceramic figurine."

I laugh, but mostly I just watch how she walks beside me like she's always belonged here. She makes this place feel less like a fortress and more like a future.

"We're having a welcoming feast tonight," I say. "Nothing too formal. Just the pack celebrating that their Alpha is finally moving in with his mate."

She halts for half a second, then looks up at me through her lashes, a grin pulling at her lips. "You know I love it when you call me that. *Mate.* Say it again."

I lean in, lips brushing her ear. "My mate."

She shivers, eyes a little glassy now. "That still gets me."

I lead her toward the market square. And fuck, I want to kiss her. Right here, in front of everyone. I want her scent on my mouth, her breath in my lungs.

The square is alive with activity. Vendors shout greetings. Kids chase each other between carts. Fresh bread, handmade knives, furs, herbs, charms—it's all here. Everything we need. We've learned to be self-sufficient. Many of us also want to live like our ancestors did... off the land, supporting one another.

"This place is perfect, and one reason I love coming here," she murmurs, eyes wide with wonder. She nudges me with a soft smile. "Well... second reason. You're the first." Then she grins. "Okay, and also because of Mikael. Your bestie hangs around here now and won't stop spilling stories about your past."

I groan, already smiling. "Yeah, well, we're going to have a little chat, the three of us, about what he can and can't reveal."

She laughs. "He told me you once tried to impress a girl by setting the training grounds on fire."

"I was fifteen," I says, dragging a hand down my face. "And it was controlled fire." I pause, then gestures ahead to change the topic. "We've got schools, a medical center, a forge, and even decided to build a library."

She tilts her head, looking absolutely adorable.

"And you're the only natural medium in this pack. We're going to need more books on ghosts," I explain.

"Gods, you're so romantic," she deadpans. "Build me a library, Daddy."

Heat flares low in my spine. I step in closer, until our bodies are almost touching. "Careful. You can't say shit like that and expect me to behave."

"Oh, is that so?" Her voice drops half an octave. "I just expect you to wait until I say when."

Fuck. Me.

She pulls back with a dangerous smirk, then strolls over to a flower stall. The old woman running it brightens immediately and starts peppering her with questions about a deceased brother who still won't leave the damn attic. I stay where I am, watching her work.

She tilts her head when listening to spirits. Softens her voice when delivering messages. Smiles with that wicked, knowing curve that says she sees things no one else can.

And for all the power humming beneath her skin, she is gentle.

Perfect here.

Perfect everywhere.

Just... perfect.

I catch her eyes across the stall, and she holds my gaze like she's tethered to it. Something invisible hums between us. Not just the soul merge. Not just the magic. But something deeper. Wilder.

She mouths, *You're staring.*

I mouth back, *I can't help it.*

She lifts a flower to her nose, sniffing it dramatically.

I raise a brow.

She smirks.

I'm already moving and heading outside until she's ready.

"You're acting strange," Rickon notes, appearing at my elbow.

"Mind your own business," I tease.

"You're completely whipped."

"Absolutely."

He laughs, shaking his head. "Never thought I'd see the day. The great Alpha Ash, brought low by a woman who talks to ghosts."

"She brought me back to life," I say simply. "She woke something in me I thought I'd lost—the desire for a future."

"That's beautiful. Also nauseating. But mostly beautiful."

Erynn returns before I can fire back, her cheeks flushed from the cold, a bouquet of frost-kissed winter roses cradled in her arms.

"The flower vendor insisted," she says, eyes sparkling as she presses her face into the blooms. "They even smell like snow."

She spins slowly, taking in the square again, where children dart between booths and old warriors haggle over honey and steel.

"I love it here already. It's so alive. The city was loud, but I still felt... alone. This feels like community."

"It is," I say, sliding an arm around her waist. She fits there like she's always belonged. "You're part of it now. The pack's been prepping for weeks. There's even a committee dedicated to making sure you feel welcome."

"You're kidding?"

"Led by Meri. She's eight. Very serious. Everyone has had to rehearse the welcome song."

"There's a song?"

"Always. We sing about everything. Victory, heartbreak, eating."

She laughs, and it lights something in my chest that still feels new. Familiar but electric.

"Show me our room?" she asks, and that little *our* sends my wolf into a purring frenzy.

"Suite," I correct, lacing our fingers together. "And gladly."

We pass through the great hall, where feast prep is already underway. Tables being arranged. Evergreens strung along the walls. The mouthwatering scent of roasted elk in the air.

The east tower suite is ready—bedroom, study, sitting area, a renovated bathroom with a soaking tub large enough to host negotiations. I watch her step into the room like she's arriving in a dream.

"This is bigger than my place," she murmurs, spinning slowly.

"Speaking of... Is Mr. Whiskers coming too?"

"Probably already here, scaring your warriors and rearranging furniture."

I draw her close, breathing her in. Just us. No distance. No schedules. No portals.

"I missed you," I murmur. "Every single day. My wolf lost his damn mind trying to get back to you."

"Just your wolf?" she teases, voice low.

"Me too. All of me."

I drown in those apple-green eyes. "I know six months isn't long, and we're still figuring all this out. But, Erynn, having you here—"

She kisses me. Fierce and certain.

"I love you too," she whispers. "Now stop being sentimental and show me that bathtub you said you installed. I want to freshen up and start anew."

"You smell delicious." Already, I'm leading her into the bathroom.

She walks the space like she's staking a claim.

Not just the wolf settling. Not just the magic balancing.

It's home.

She's home.

We are.

She circles back and wraps her arms around me, pressing her forehead to mine.

"We did it," she says softly.

"We did," I echo.

"No more goodbyes. No more watching you disappear through a portal. No more nights alone."

"Never again."

Outside, the snow falls. Inside, we start a new life.

Tonight, she's celebrated.

Tomorrow, we build.

But this moment, right now?

My mate is here.

My wolf is calm.

And the impossible thing we've become?

It's exactly what I never knew I needed.